D0337763

OCT 29 '97

The Curses of
Third Uncle

PAUL YEE

The Curses of
Third Uncle

James Lorimer & Company, Publishers
Toronto 1986

Canadian Cataloguing in Publication Data

Yee, Paul
    The curses of third uncle
(Adventures in Canadian history)
ISBN 0-88862-910-9 (bound). — ISBN 0-88862-909-5 (pbk.)
I. Besco, Don.   II. Title   III. Series.
PS8597.E3C87 1986   jC813'.54   C86-094415-8
PZ7.Y43Cu 1986

Copyright © 1986 by Paul Yee. All rights reserved. No part of this book may be
reproduced or transmitted in any form or by any means, electronic or mechanical,
including photocopying, or by any information storage and retrieval system, without
permission in writing from the publisher.

0-88862-909-5 paper
0-88862-910-9 cloth

Design: Dreadnaught
Illustrations: Don Besco

**Teacher's guide available from publisher.
Write to address below.**

An Adventure in Canadian History Book

James Lorimer & Company, Publishers
Egerton Ryerson Memorial Building
35 Britain St.
Toronto, Ontario M5A 1R7

Printed and bound in Canada

Dedicated to my aunt, Lillian Ho Wong (1895-1985),
whose stories and memories inspired this book.

ACKNOWLEDGEMENTS

My thanks to Judy Chan, Jim Wong-Chu, Dierdre Bradshaw and Ken Young for many different kinds of assistance. The staff at Revelstoke Museum and Glacier National Park Interpretive Centre were also helpful, as were Sharon Walliser and Don Lee and their students at Hastings Elementary. Finally, this book has benefitted greatly under the guidance of my editors, Shelley Tanaka and Linda Sheppard.

This book was published in celebration of Vancouver's Centennial with the financial assistance of the Vancouver Centennial Commission.

VANCOUVER

city of the century

1

"I wish I had a birthday every week," Lillian thought dreamily as she poked her head out the streetcar window and felt the wind on her face. "If Papa sat with me just once a week, I'd never complain about homework or sewing or looking after Baby. I wish this ride would last forever!"

She looked out over the glistening water of Vancouver harbour. The gleaming hull of a great ocean liner cut like a knife through the green-blue water. Trails of smoke drifted up from the ship's smokestacks towards the distant mountains that ringed the inlet.

Lillian leaned happily into her father and inhaled his clean soap scent. Papa looked as if he was dreaming, too. The streetcar had passed through the downtown and now it coasted by lonely stands of tall trees and grand-looking houses enclosed by white picket fences. The newly cleared West End was filling so quickly with homes and roads that it was hard to believe this had all been thick forest just twenty-five years earlier. Lillian saw the park bridge draw closer and closer across the sparkling waters. Then she could make out rowboats at the pier and the gravelly seawall path.

The streetcar came to a stop, and Lillian and Papa stepped off. Instantly her heart tightened like a fist. Three Chinese stood out from the crowd, with long pigtails dangling down behind their Chinese-style jackets. All the men in Chinatown seemed to wear the same clothes — except for her papa and a few other "modern" Chinese who wore western suits and boots.

"Come on!" Lillian glanced nervously at the Chinese and tugged at Papa. Families were hurrying across the bridge into the huge forests and fields of Stanley Park. The rich aroma of heavy pine trees filled her nose. She was anxious to disappear into the park.

But it was too late.

"Wei! Ho Jin Chong!" She heard voices call out to Papa. "Wei!"

The three men came running over with happy smiles across their tanned faces. "What a coincidence to bump into you here!"

"Oh, it's you fellows!" boomed Papa's deep voice. "You lazy worms! You've come to the park, too, have you?"

As people turned and stared, Lillian's face reddened. She wondered if she and Papa could go anywhere without meeting someone from Chinatown. She wished the ground beneath would open up and swallow them all!

"Today, you're taking a rest-day?" one man asked Papa. He mopped at the sweat bubbling on his brow.

"That's right," replied Papa. "My eldest daughter, it's her birthday today, so we came out for a walk."

Lillian drew a tense breath. "Hello, Elder Uncle. Hello, Younger Uncle," she muttered. Like all Chinese children, Lillian addressed men acquaintances as "uncle" even when there was no blood relation.

She tried to pull her father away, but the newcomers ignored her. She stepped back and smoothed her dress. These men are ruining my day, she fumed. We didn't come all this way just to stand around with them! Can't they at least step into the shade where people won't see them?

She glared at the men, but they were too busy talking. She itched to walk away, but knew that would reflect badly on Papa.

"Any news from Canton?"

"I hear the Empire's getting nervous."

"Extra troops are on alert!"

"What about you, Jin? Are you scared?"

Scared? Lillian stiffened. What could scare Papa?

But her father just smiled. "You believe everything those sailors say?"

"No, listen to me, Old Ho!" The men's voices dropped low and urgent. "This time, it could be dangerous! The revolution, it's serious now!"

"You should get out while you can!"

"The Empire is still strong. Don't underestimate them!"

Lillian's hands still fidgeted, but now she listened hard. Then one man nudged another as his eyes flickered towards her. Quickly they changed the topic.

"Has it ever been so hot in July?"

"Look how clear and blue the sky is. Isn't it pretty?"

Lillian pretended to yawn, but she seethed inside. Now she would never know what they were afraid of! What was this word revolution? If she had a pair of scissors, she'd run up and cut off their pigtails! Snip, snip! Then they wouldn't look so strange. Then maybe the whites wouldn't hate the Chinese so much.

Suddenly a clang sounded from the streetcar and it began to move.

"Ai-yah!" shouted the men. "The car's starting! Wei, wait! Wait for us!"

The trio dashed off in a panic, shouting and waving their soft hats like flags, while their pigtails tossed madly behind them. The entire carload of passengers turned at the commotion and Lillian groaned. Everyone was laughing at them! The men looked like three storm-frightened pigs charging about. Didn't they know anything?

Papa waved goodbye and shouted, "Careful! Tomorrow I'll come look for you! We'll talk then!"

But already Lillian was walking away. Sometimes that Papa of hers was a real donkey!

"Ah-Lai, wait!" called Papa. He came running up to match her pace. "How strange to bump into those fellows!" he mused to himself. "I wonder if they knew we were coming here."

When he reached out to take Lillian's hand, she shook him off angrily.

"Oh, that's right, you're a year older today," exclaimed Papa. "Too big to hold my hand. How old are you now?"

Work it out yourself, she thought furiously. It's 1909 today and I was born in 1895. Simple arithmetic makes me fourteen!

Every birthday Papa asked Lillian her age, and it always annoyed her. Papa rarely talked to her, yet she was the first-born, so how could he forget? She had tried to make him notice her, but he was always too busy. Until today. When Papa had announced Stanley Park, she had leapt for joy because they had never gone out alone. To her the outing became a reward, a prize — and maybe even an apology for all those words he had left unsaid over the years.

They walked in silence through the trees, past picnickers and then over a grassy knoll into a harbour breeze. Though long beds of sunny flowers stretched over the park lawns, Lillian couldn't smell their fragrance. Instead her nose wrinkled at the smell of salt and seaweed. A gust lifted her skirts and Papa clapped his hand over his hat. They turned and trotted down towards the Oval playground where bagpipes were wailing. She read the banner: "Scottish Society Highland Games" and saw a table laden with trophies and plaques.

Then the kilts caught her eye. They looked funny, but at least they were cool, she thought. What a good idea for men to wear skirts! She giggled as she pictured Papa wearing one. Wouldn't that set Chinatown talking?

The heat and sweat clung stickily under Lillian's knee-length skirts, and she shook them out to air them. Despite the hot mid-day sun, the women wore long dresses that swept the ground. But some of them carried parasols, and their hats had generous brims.

Lillian looked around for familiar faces. She knew she wouldn't find any of her Chinese classmates here, not at the picnic of a group as proud as the Scottish Society. She wondered if Susan McKay, who sat behind her in class, would dare say hello to her here in public. For this special occasion, the boys wore starched shirts atop their knickers, while the girls glimmered in snowy pinafores.

If she weren't Chinese and her family wasn't so poor, Lillian thought enviously, she would be wearing a dress like that, too!

For the first event, logs the size of telegraph poles lay on the ground. The first contestant, a red-bearded man who was as thick and stocky as a barrel, walked over and squatted to lift one end of the log. Slowly he raised it over his head, rose to his feet and then began to walk under it, bracing and pushing it up with each step. When he reached the other end, the log stood almost upright.

Then, with a ferocious grunt, he lifted the log into the air. It sprang up, pointing skywards. Lillian's hand flew to her mouth. The crowd gasped and moved back. The log swayed in the air while the man fought to keep it aloft.

"Throw it, throw it!" the crowd chanted. "Let it go!"

With a battle cry the man heaved the log, and it somersaulted through the air. It fell with a dull thud and the officials rushed up to measure the toss. Papa was applauding and calling out, "Bravo! Bravo! Good throw!" with the crowd.

He grinned at Lillian and she began to clap, too. But she felt people turning and staring. A surge of panic ripped through her. Were they too conspicuous?

But this time she didn't care. They were dressed the same as everyone else. They spoke English. Why shouldn't they clap and shout? Papa could probably toss the log farther than any man there! Lillian looked proudly up at her father and clapped even louder.

Papa nudged her shoulder. "Come on, let's go. There's something I want you to see."

"What, Papa?" She hurried to keep up as they strode across the meadow. "Where are we going?"

"To see something special. Something you've never seen before!"

"What is it? Is it in the zoo?"

"That's where we'll start!" he announced.

Start what? Lillian skipped circles around her father even as they walked. Papa never teased her like this!

"Look! Monkeys!" She ran up to the cage where they

leapt and swung about. She studied their tiny faces and tried to count them, but already they had darted away. She felt Papa come up behind her. "Is this what you wanted me to see?"

"These little fellows?" Papa shook his head. "No, not them. But wait, this is for you."

He had gone to the peanut vendor, and now he handed a bag of nuts to her. "This year, your birthday, this is all I have. Your papa's sorry." He looked down at his feet.

Lillian stared at her father. Never before had Papa apologized to her! On her last birthday, he had tossed a fountain pen on the table and muttered, "For you." But this year he had taken her out, and now they were actually talking!

"Thank you, Papa," she finally managed. "Thank you very much."

But he wasn't listening. He was sniffing at the breeze and watching people leap gleefully back and forth over the little brook that trickled down to the seal pond. At the bandstand, a uniformed band struck up a tune, but immediately the flock of seals started to howl. Papa burst out laughing and led the way into the forest.

Lillian followed. "What are we—"

"Shush! Or you'll scare it away!"

The trail curled through the dense bush. Under the shade of the trees, the air hung cool and fragrant. Lillian looked up to the treetops to see the sunlight sparkling through like flashes of jewellery. Around them, birds chirped and leaves rustled. They walked and walked.

"Look!" Papa suddenly whispered. "Over there!"

Lillian caught her breath. It was a peacock! Its sharp crested head rose stiffly over a speckled brown body dwarfed by the heavy, broom-like tail. Lillian had never seen a real peacock before! It looked like some ancient queen, tottering along with head held high and a long wispy gown trailing behind. Papa crept quickly after it.

"Wah! Look at that! Ah-Lai, come quickly! Hurry!"

A glorious semi-circle of colour had suddenly blossomed in the middle of the trail. The peacock had turned and spread open its fantail. The greens and golds of the softly waving feathers caught flashes of sun and leapt out at Lillian.

"Isn't that beautiful?" Papa breathed, and she nodded. It was magical!

"Take a close look, Ah-Lai," he continued softly. "It's a sign of good fortune to see a peacock open its fan."

"Really?" Lillian was totally enchanted.

"They say it's revealed only in the presence of deserving people. Have you been good lately?"

She gulped. "Well..."

Papa chuckled. "I hope there's enough good luck for both of us!"

After the peacock had strutted off, Papa stood up and moved on. Lillian followed behind, fascinated at how graceful and perfect the peacock was. And she had seen one! If good luck was coming her way, she wondered what to wish for. A new dress? New shoes?

They emerged from the forest at a calm lake of cool clear water and waded into it. Back on shore, they nibbled on the peanuts. Papa stretched his long body out and closed his eyes against the sun. His face relaxed and Lillian studied his high broad forehead and the jagged scar running down one cheek. Had Papa got that cut on one of his trips up north? Papa never said much about those journeys, and Lillian never dared to ask about them. All she knew was that they were important to him, just as important as the meetings he was always attending in Chinatown.

Lillian sat quietly, glad to be beside her papa. His powerful hands lay gently clasped and he wriggled his pale hairy toes in the breeze.

"This is *my* papa," she told herself proudly. "He takes me out and talks to me. We saw a peacock together. My father shares his good luck with me!"

* * * *

Lillian sighed when she stepped off the streetcar. This time it was Papa who had to pull her along. Home was only two short blocks away, but Lillian dragged her heels over the wooden sidewalks and looked longingly at the store window displays. Two times Papa had to call out for her to hurry.

After crossing Hastings Street, they were in Chinatown. Things didn't appear greatly different from the street behind them. The glass windows shone, the buildings were brick and three storeys high, and the storekeepers hung fresh foods and general goods out in the open. Of course, all the store signs were painted in Chinese, but a few had English names. And here the streets were crowded because Sunday's half-day of work set the men of Chinatown free for one afternoon.

"Don't tell Mama about the peanuts," Papa warned as they entered the store with "Hing Kee, Merchant Tailors" emblazoned on the window in great gilt letters.

Lillian nodded. Mama watched every penny in the house with hawk-sharp eyes, and she frowned on snacks. Lillian wasn't going to give her any excuse to spoil her perfect day!

The rows of sewing machines in the shop stood silent. Two men were playing dominoes, Ah-Ming was tuning his bamboo flute, and others were writing and reading. Freshly washed clothes hung from poles propped between the partitions, dripping onto newspapers spread beneath. Papa's eleven employees boarded in the store, where bunkbeds and sawhorse plank beds stood in the back room. At night they were joined by others who worked at the nearby sawmills and hotels.

"You're back already?" A grey-haired man groped his way along the wall to them. Despite the summer weather, Blind-Eye wore several layers of shirts and sweaters over his thin wiry frame. He claimed he always felt cold. Papa said that being blind, poor and alone in a strange country had made Blind-Eye unusually worried. The two men had originally met on the long boat trip coming to Canada. Then, several years later, Blind-Eye had stumbled in to beg for help. A foundry explosion had robbed him of his eyesight and he couldn't find work anywhere. Ever since then, Papa had let him eat and sleep with his workers for free.

"Guess what we saw?" Lillian skipped rings around Blind-Eye and almost tripped him. She had been avoiding him lately because she couldn't stand listening to his stories anymore. Sometimes he bragged about how his family used to raise the fattest pigs and grow the sweetest sugar cane in their home county. Other times he told of the magic spells and mighty emperors and beautiful women of ancient China. It sounded like fairy tales to Lillian, but the rest of Chinatown's children loved his stories.

"Be careful!" called out Papa. "Fetch a chair for him!"

"We saw a peacock open its fan!" Lillian announced while she helped the blind man to a seat. "It was so beautiful!"

"That should bring you lots of luck, then," Blind-Eye commented. "Did you know it's good fortune?"

"Yes, Papa told me! We crept after it in the forest until —"

"Wei, Blind-Eye!" Papa interrupted. "Did you bring home a newspaper today?"

The story-teller frequented Chinatown's tea houses, where he begged for meals to lessen his burden on the Hos. In the restaurants he would find a corner and pull out his wooden clappers. His fingers made them dance and click, and once the rhythm was set, Blind-Eye would perform a story. Sometimes the customers dropped the daily newspaper instead of coins into his lap.

The old man nodded and held out the pages. "Anxious about things in China, are you?"

"Just a bit, just a bit." And then Papa headed upstairs.

Lillian twirled towards the kitchen which was between the storefront and the sleeping room at the rear. The aromas of dinner rose and her stomach rumbled. Lately she was always hungry, no matter how much she ate. She had been growing so rapidly in the past few months. Her body stuck out awkwardly from clothes that were always too small.

The big round table was already set with chopsticks and spoons. All the stores and factories in Chinatown fed their employees, and Uncle Jing, a friend from Papa's village, cooked rice twice a day. He prepared enough for the Hos, too, and carried the trays of food upstairs. Later Lillian brought the empty dishes downstairs and helped wash them.

Uncle Jing was immersed in a cloud of steam as pots bubbled before him. The gigantic cast-iron wok hissed and crackled.

"What are we eating tonight?" Lillian asked jauntily. From behind him, she ducked from one side to the other to peer at the cooking.

"Stop playing around here!" barked out Uncle Jing.

"Go and get ready for dinner!"

Lillian hopped off, humming and singing to herself. Upstairs, Winnie and Nellie, her ten- and eleven-year-old sisters, sat at the sitting-room table with Mama, facing a mountain of shirts. When the contracts came in, Papa's workers sewed denim pants for the department stores and Chinese-style clothes for sale throughout British Columbia. Chugging like train engines and guided by nimble fingers, the foot-powered sewing machines hemmed the ragged edges of cloth and shaped them into garments. Then the assembly line led upstairs to Mama and the girls for button-holing and fine-stitching.

Lillian crept up behind Nellie and jabbed her sides. Nellie squealed and leapt up while Lillian spun away, laughing at her outraged sister.

"Watch out, stupid! You almost put the needle through my thumb!"

"So what?" Lillian had filled her mug with water and was drinking greedily. Streams of water trickled out the side of her mouth.

"Look at the pig wet herself all over," snickered Winnie.

Lillian drew her cuff across her mouth. "You're just mad because you didn't get to go out," she taunted. "You'll never guess what we saw! Never in a million years!"

"Who wants to play guessing games with you?" sniffed Nellie.

"We have work to do," chimed in Winnie.

"Go on, guess! I'll give you a clue. It's something to do with good luck!"

She leaned on the high-backed wooden chair and waited. The room was almost filled by the long table around which the family ate and worked. Jars and tins cluttered the shelves by the little stove, calendars decorated the walls, and a Chinese tea basket sat on an upturned crate. In the corner stood heavy bolts of cloth. The windows overlooked Chinatown's main street and admitted ample amounts of light.

Mama stood up to fold the shirts. "Ah-Lai, why do you make trouble?" she cut in wearily. "Don't you have to help, too? You think the work will get done on its own?"

Mama was slightly built, and the long western skirts she wore made her look even thinner. But her glossy black hair was pulled into a firm bun behind piercing eyes and a mouth that always seemed to be set in a frown.

"Uncle Jing told me to set the table for dinner." Lillian hardly felt like sewing now. Her birthday was nothing special to Mama. Today was just another day with another shipment of sewing that had to be finished. Poor Mama, Lillian sighed. Too bad Papa never took her to Stanley Park. "Here," she offered suddenly. "I'll take Baby."

She untied the carrying sash that held Ruth to Mama's back. The baby slept soundly. Papa sat in his favourite chair reading the newspaper. Lillian took Ruth into her parents' bedroom, cooing and kissing her, and placed her on the bed. The diaper was wet, and she reached for a fresh one. If she took extra care, she might not even wake Ruth while she changed her. When she finished, she peered in the dresser mirror and saw her own face break into a smile. She felt like leaping up and bouncing around on the soft mattress. It was her birthday!

When she returned to the sitting room, Uncle Jing had already brought up the dinner. But Papa was still hidden behind his thin wall of newsprint. Every night the children sat and fussed at the table until Mama and Papa were both seated.

Finally Mama pulled him over and spooned out bowlfuls of rice. When she sat down, the sisters quickly murmured, "Papa, Mama, please eat," as they did before every meal, and reached for their soup spoons.

"What's this?" Mama removed the lids and peered through the steam. "It's barbequed spareribs!"

Lillian's mouth watered. What a treat!

"I wonder where this came from," Mama muttered, looking suspiciously at Papa.

"I told Jing to buy some," said Papa. "Today, it's Ah-Lai's birthday."

Mama let out a worried sigh. "Jin, if you buy meat for every birthday, we'll soon have to sell one of these girls."

Lillian reached eagerly for a glistening piece of meat. She sucked the juicy sweet bone and caught her mother glaring at her.

"What are you eating so noisily for?" Mama

demanded. "You're not a pig, you know."

Leave me alone, Lillian pouted silently. Be nice to me. It's my birthday.

Suddenly one of the workers called from the stairwell. "Wei! Ho Jin Chong! There's someone come to see you!"

Papa frowned and left the table. When he did not return immediately, Mama selected some choice pieces of meat and placed them on his bowl.

"Wei, pick that up!" Mama pointed to a few grains of rice Lillian had spilled. "Do you know how much hard labour it takes to put a single grain of rice in your bowl?"

Then Papa came upstairs and disappeared swiftly into the bedroom. When he still did not come to the table, Mama sighed and went to see him.

"You only get two more," Winnie called out as Lillian reached for the bowl of spareribs again.

"We've counted," announced Nellie. "Everyone gets two more. Fair's fair!"

"But it's my birth —" Lillian started, but her mother's voice slashed through the walls.

"Going? Going where? What do you mean, you can't tell me?" Mama's voice grew shrill. "Tell me where you're going!"

Lillian's day deflated like a punctured ball. Papa had to go away again! Every time this happened, he and Mama fought and fought. He would be gone anywhere from a few days to several weeks. Oh, Papa, Lillian cursed, not now! Why did you pick tonight to go?

"No, you can't go! I forbid it!" Mama shouted. "Think of the children, fool! You have another one coming, do you know?"

Then Ruth awoke and started howling. Lillian broke free of her anger and leapt to bring her from the bedroom into the sitting room. But Ruth wailed heatedly and beat her tiny fists into her sister's face.

"Come on, stop crying, stop crying." She rocked her sister impatiently as the shouting in the bedroom became louder. "Be good, please?"

"What if something happens?" demanded Mama. "This time it could be dangerous, do you know that?"

Lillian's face whitened. Dangerous? The men at the park had used that word! Then Mama stormed out of the bedroom. Her darkened face was twisted with rage.

"Here, give me the baby, you useless thing!" she snarled. "Ai-yah, can't you even look after one baby?"

When she came over, Lillian saw wet eyes and trembling lips. But her mama never cried!

Suddenly scattered moments from the day collected and darkened in her mind. The men at the park. They had warned Papa to be careful, about that revolution. Blind-Eye had asked if Papa was anxious about the news. And who would call on Papa during the dinner hour? It must have been bad news. Very bad.

"You, Ah-Lai! You, you stupid thing!" Mama scowled. "Your papa wants to talk to you."

Me? Lillian edged into the bedroom. What did I do? She stared at a crack running through the wallpaper.

"Papa?" Her voice wavered. He was throwing clothes into a travelling bag, his back towards her.

He grunted and turned around. "You're almost an adult now, Ah-Lai," he stated curtly. "You don't need to play so much. Whatever your mother says, you obey her, understand?"

Lillian looked down at the splintery floorboards. Was this all he wanted — just to lecture her? She bit her lips.

"You're the eldest. You watch over your sisters," he continued. "If I hear of trouble, I'll whip you thoroughly when I come home. Hear that?"

A voice inside her head shouted, "Ask him where he's going! Ask him about the danger! Why is this trip so different?" But she just nodded.

Papa clapped his hat on his head, seized the satchel and stomped down the stairs. When the front door slammed, Lillian began trembling. Tears gushed from her eyes. Quickly she stuffed a fist into her mouth so that Mama wouldn't hear her.

The word "dangerous" stabbed into her heart. "Oh, Papa," she moaned. "Where are you going?"

2

"YOU still haven't heard from your papa yet?" asked Emily Kwan. She rolled her eyes in disbelief.

Lillian shook her head.

"He's been gone for five months, hasn't he?" Emily persisted.

Lillian tightened her scarf and marched quickly ahead on the wooden sidewalk. Inside her mind boiled. Why couldn't Emily leave her alone? Everyone in Chinatown was already laughing at her family. The Hos haven't anything to eat, the Hos are out of business. Look what happens when the man of the house runs off!

The heated thoughts warmed her briefly. Never before had December been so cold in Vancouver. In the sun-filled mornings, the roads lay frosted with a layer of glittering white. By the end of school, the windows in the stuffy classroom were coated with a thin slick of ice on the outside. Lillian's entire body tensed against the stinging chill. The cold air invading her lungs seemed to seep into her empty stomach, too.

"Lillian, wait!" called Emily. "What's your hurry? Can't wait to start your homework, is that it?"

Lillian gritted her teeth. Emily was supposed to be her best friend, yet every day she grew more irritating. Yesterday she had wanted to go skating.

"I can't go," Lillian had replied.

"I'll buy your ticket," her friend had offered.

Still she had shaken her head.

"What's the matter?" Emily had demanded. "You don't want to do anything these days!"

"I have to be at home!" Lillian had cried out. "Just in case something happens to Mama."

"You worry too much," her friend had retorted. "You always used to complain about your mother's nagging!"

Now Emily pranced up with a glint in her eyes. "Guess what I heard from my mother!"

When Lillian ignored her, she blurted out, "She said... well, you know I don't believe her, but... but she said your papa's head was chopped off in China!"

Lillian sighed. It was just another in the endless stream of rumours about Papa.

"So what do you think of that?" trumpeted Emily, as wisps of steam danced from her mouth.

"Papa didn't go to China," Lillian declared.

"How do you know? He's never written!"

"So? That doesn't mean anything!" Lillian marched

ahead defiantly. "Besides, why would Papa go to China?"

"To fight in that revolution of his!"

Revolution? Lillian turned quickly to her friend. "Emily, what's the revolution?"

"I don't know!" Emily shrugged.

"But you just said it."

"So? I hear all kinds of words from my mother. Why don't you ask someone else?"

Lillian shook her head. "Even Blind-Eye won't tell me. Everything's a big secret."

"I told you your papa was involved," crowed Emily. "My mother said —"

"Stop it!" screamed Lillian. She put her hands over her ears. "You're crazy! Your mother's crazy! I don't want to hear any more!" Then she spun around and ran down the hill towards home.

"I hate you, Papa!" she cried as the buildings hurtled by. "I hate you a million times! Why aren't you home? Why don't you write? Don't you care about us anymore? Where *are* you?"

She flew across the road without looking and turned the corner. She burst through the doors of Hing Kee and thundered upstairs into the sitting room. Winnie and Nellie sat at the table copying sentences into their notebooks. Beside them, Mama was unrolling her last bolt of cloth for a jacket that she would try to sell. With one glance at her eldest daughter she shook her head.

"Look at your face, stupid girl," she sighed. "Ink all

over. Do you use your nose for a pen?"

Lillian wrinkled her nose. Was there ink on her face? She was more worried about her mother. Mama was always nagging at her, but lately her voice had weakened. When she scolded now, it snaked out in a low, deadly whisper.

Lillian rubbed her face absently and went to the cookie tins on the shelf. She shook them, but found each empty. She rummaged among the other cannisters. Maybe someone had called on Mama today and brought treats.

"Nothing's there, don't bother looking," Mama informed her. "Ai-yah, wash your face before I twist your ear off."

Lillian picked up her washcloth and peered in the mirror. An ordinary face stared back. The two braids that pulled her long hair back revealed large healthy ears — signs of a long life, according to Papa. Her father believed in all kinds of good-luck omens: the colour red, rainbows, and peacocks' fans. At the memory of the peacock, the face in the mirror brightened.

"Papa *will* be back soon," Lillian told herself firmly.

"Come here and hold the cloth while I cut it," ordered Mama.

Lillian tried to look eager. She wanted to help, especially now that Papa was gone, but Mama never seemed satisfied. She would always find mistakes in Lillian's work. Mama's face looked peaked and haggard, and her tummy bulged noticeably. Soon there would be another mouth to feed. Lillian hoped for a brother, because that would make Mama smile.

All of Chinatown liked boys better. Third Uncle labelled girls as "seet boon foh" — no profit goods — that were totally useless. Boys would be sent to school while girls were often kept at home. Some of the richer families had servant-girls who were no older than Lillian.

"What's that?" Mama looked up suddenly.

Lillian tilted her head and heard rapping at the door. As she sprang down the stairs she wondered who it might be. People usually walked straight into the store. No one ever knocked. The main floor was empty. Ever since the store had stopped operating, the boarders ate on their own outside.

She opened the door. There stood a young man, shivering in a short padded jacket.

"Please, is this where Mr. Ho Jin Chong lives?" he asked.

From his accent and shiny shoes Lillian saw at once that he was city-folk and newly arrived. All newcomers seemed to come to Canada wearing a pair of new leather shoes, whether they wore Chinese or western pants.

She nodded. "But my father's not at home."

The young man paused. "May I come in? I'm not used to this cold."

"Yes, yes, come in." She looked closely as he stepped

inside and took off his cap. Like Papa, he kept no pigtail. His shoulders were wide, and shiny pimples speckled his face ruthlessly.

"My surname is Lam," he said. "Your mother, is she home?"

"She's upstairs." Lillian walked him to the back and up the stairwell. She almost ran because her heart was pounding madly. Perhaps this was news about Papa! "Mama, this is Mr. Lam. He's looking for Papa!"

Mama looked the man up and down. "Is that so?" Her voice strengthened immediately. "Ah-Lai, you and your sisters, go to your room now."

"Mrs. Ho?" The young man bowed politely. "You're well?"

Mama nodded curtly. "You wish to see my husband. What is the nature of your business?" She shut the door behind the girls. Once inside their room, Lillian huddled at the door to catch every word.

"Did he bring anything to eat?" whispered Nellie.

"What's he here for?" Winnie breathed into her other ear.

"Shush!" Lillian shook her head furiously. "Be quiet!"

Lam fumbled with his answer. "Your husband usually wrote to us in China once a month. For a long while he hasn't written. I came over to see if all was in order."

"What did Jin write to you about?" asked Mama.

Lam groped for words. "It was... it was about money... and our association..."

MALASPINA UNIVERSITY-COLLEGE LIBRARY

"What association?" demanded Mama. Lillian felt sorry for the man. If he were older, Mama wouldn't dare be so blunt.

Lillian strained to hear the muffled answer, and then she heard Mama's voice cut harshly through the wall. "My husband left town five months ago. He didn't tell me where he was going. I don't know where he is now."

"Didn't he send you letters?" asked Lam.

"No. He knows that I cannot read."

"Has anyone else in town heard from him?"

"No."

"Did he say when he would return?"

"No, he just takes care of himself," replied Mama bitterly. "I'm sorry, but I'm busy. I have a baby to look after."

Lillian blinked in amazement. Never before had she heard Mama treat a visitor so rudely.

"Wait, please," begged the stranger. "This is important! I have to find him. It's a matter of life and death!"

Lillian sucked in a breath.

"It's life and death here, too," retorted Mama. "Jin runs off to play revolution and abandons us without money or means. I have children to feed, young man. I have a baby coming! Why don't you go ask at the Athletic Club? The men there are ready to fight the Empire!"

Lam turned to leave. "I should go —"

"It's easy for men in Canada to toy with revolution!"

Mama shouted. "There aren't any armies here to fight against!"

"Sorry to have disturbed you."

Suddenly Mama's voice lost its harshness. "Is my husband in danger? Please tell me!"

"I don't know, Mrs. Ho," Lam replied earnestly. "If I learn anything, I'll contact you immediately."

"You sailed all the way across the Pacific just to ask about Jin?" Mama asked sarcastically.

"No, not at all," the visitor answered. "Dr. Sun is coming, and I'm to see that things are safe here."

After Lam's departure, the girls trooped back to the sitting room. Mama had resumed sewing, but when the sisters saw her frowning darkly, they worked in silence for a while. Finally Lillian asked the most harmless question she could think of.

"What association did Mr. Lam belong to?"

"Don't you mind." Mama did not even look up.

Lillian opened her copybook but the lines blurred before her eyes. Papa's China friends were worried. Something *had* happened to him. Money was involved, so of course they were concerned. No one knew where Papa was. Now the revolution sounded like war! And who was this Dr. Sun? He must be important if Lam had come over just to make sure things were safe. Life and death? Lillian shuddered.

"Is Blind-Eye back yet?" asked Mama. He bought the groceries now, since married women traditionally were not allowed to step out alone. "He's never around when I need him!"

The front door below slammed. "Perhaps that's him."

They heard the work tables rattle as someone stumbled into them.

Lillian winced. It was Third Uncle, Papa's younger brother. He had come from China to live with them six years ago. Lillian had never seen him do a day's work. His footsteps sounded on the stairs and then he swaggered in. The smells of stale tobacco and alcohol filled the air. She quickly opened a textbook. Maybe if she read hard enough, she wouldn't even know he was there!

"Why don't you turn on the lights downstairs? Damn nearly killed myself!" he cried.

"Saving money," Mama replied curtly. Then she inquired politely, "Have you eaten yet?"

Third Uncle ignored her. "I saw Fat Old Wong at the tea house today," he announced. "I'm selling the sewing machines to him."

"What?" Mama's eyebrows flew up as she spun around. "What did you say?"

He saw the scissors gleaming in Mama's hands and faltered. "Not much, Sister-in-law. I ... I'm selling the sewing machines and ... and I'm sending you all back to China."

Lillian gasped. Sending them back? But she and her sisters had been born here. She had never even been to China!

"Who told you to do so?" demanded Mama.

"No . . . no one," stammered Third Uncle. Lillian saw his left cheek twitching madly.

"I tell you clearly now," Mama stated slowly, the scissors dancing in her hand as she walked up to him. "This store, it belongs to your brother. It's not yours. You don't have a penny in this business. You have no right to sell anything, not even one slender pin!"

Third Uncle had retreated to the doorway. His bloodshot eyes bulged in his sallow face. Although he was younger than Papa, his sunken chest and stooped shoulders made him look like a withered old man.

"Damn! Elder Brother's been gone five months!" he spat out. "I'm the head of this family now. He could be dead and we wouldn't know!"

In a breath, Mama's free hand slashed across his face. Lillian jumped at the crack of the slap.

"You hear me good," Mama hissed. "Jin isn't here at home, but he's not dead yet!"

"You stinking cow!" Third Uncle screamed. "You dare touch me. Why, I'll . . ." He raised an arm over his scarlet face to strike back, but Lillian rushed over. If he touched Mama she would throw him down the stairs herself! Third Uncle looked at the two females glowering at him and dropped back.

"You're just women, you remember that! Women are cursed, they're useless! Wait until you're back in China! Then you'll see! You'll have nothing! You'll be nothing!"

With a string of foul mutterings, he turned and stomped down the stairs. Again he crashed into the work tables, but this time he toppled them over in a furious clatter. Then the door slammed.

Mama moved slowly to the table. Her face was drained of colour and her breathing wheezed loudly. Lillian's heart ached. She wanted to throw her arms around her mother and hug her tightly. Mama stood like a statue.

"Are we really going back to China?" Nellie spoke up from her corner, clear as a bell.

"No..." Mama murmured. Then her voice hardened. "Yes, it's so. We'll have to go back."

"But what about Papa?" Lillian asked in alarm. "What happens when he comes back?" Leaving Canada was like saying Papa would never return. And that couldn't be true!

Mama shrugged. "Then we'll all come back here. Who knows? At least we'll have food to eat in China."

"I don't want to go to China," Lillian stated defiantly.

"Me, neither," chimed in Nellie. "I want to stay here."

"Stay here and starve? Is that what you want?" Their mother's voice turned bitter. "There's not even enough to pay rent. How am I to manage? You tell me, how am I to manage? Have you ways of bringing in money? Have you? That's what we need now! Money!"

The children fell silent. Mama had never raved at them about money like this.

"But the boarders pay rent, don't they?" persisted Lillian.

"Oh, you're a smart one, aren't you?" sniffed Mama. "You think it's enough?"

"So we'll earn some money!" Lillian continued desperately. "We'll just have to earn some more money!"

"Earn some more money, earn some more money," Mama mimicked. "Easy to say, isn't it? All you have is a mouth!"

"I never said it was easy," protested Lillian. "I just —"

"Oh, that's right! You're always right, aren't you? If you're so smart, why don't you do something about it?"

"Okay, I will!" Lillian leapt to her feet and ran to the stairs. "I'll show you," she shouted furiously. "Just wait! I'll show you!"

Outside the frosty air cooled her rage only slightly. She dodged and twisted her way through the passersby. Men hurried by with their hands thrust deep into pockets. Lillian crossed the road and headed towards False Creek. The brick buildings lined the street snugly. Stores occupied the main floor, restaurants took some second storeys, and hostels and meeting halls filled the upper levels. At the end of the street were two noisy sawmills where the waters floated in logs.

That stupid mother of mine, Lillian raged. I'm not going to China! Not where farmers sell their daughters for money. Not where rats as big as cats run wild in the countryside, and women totter around on bound feet the size of teacups. I'm not going! Somehow I'll bring money home so Mama can't force me to go.

A minute later Lillian arrived at Ying Chong, the biggest tailor firm in Chinatown. She stopped at the door. What would she say? She almost turned back, but the thought of those huge rats steeled her.

She pushed at the door and went in. The clickety-clack of foot treadles was familiar and loud. Lillian spotted Fat Old Wong at the back and walked towards him past rows of tables. She was sure that he wanted to buy Papa's equipment just to reduce the competition for business.

Fat Old Wong was hunched over his bookkeeping. One pudgy hand sent the abacus beads flying, while the other brushed numbers into a thick ledger book of rice paper. He wore a padded jacket of brocaded silk and a thick furry cap. Lillian stared fixedly at him until he grunted at her.

"Elder Uncle," she started, "is there any hand-sewing work to send out? I came to ask if —"

"Handwork? What handwork?" he snarled. "For you penniless beggars? You'll take my garments and go out and sell them!"

Silence fell over the room like a heavy blanket. Lillian turned in a daze and stumbled towards the door. Her face burned. Poor folks shouldn't expect to receive any respect, Mama always said. Wait until you had money or education. Then people would listen to you.

But Lillian couldn't wait. The Hing Kee store was out of business, Mama was expecting a baby, and now Third Uncle wanted to send them to China. The only way to stay was to find work for money. And she would. If she gave up now, Mama might be forced to sell Ruth!

"Stupid donkey!" she swore, thinking of Fat Old

Wong. "I should've said, 'You think we'd try and sell *your* ragged clothes? Who'd buy them? They're so shoddy I couldn't even give them away!'"

Lillian turned down Shanghai Alley. She wasn't going home until she found something! Lights glowed from behind the windows and storefronts that opened onto the narrow street. Men were streaming towards the Chinese Theatre for the early evening opera performance.

A wagonload of heavy urns and sacks of rice thundered over the cobblestones. Lillian jumped away from the curb. Angry voices cursed the driver and yelled for him to slow down. The horses whinnied and snorted out thick clouds while the driver hurled insults back.

One block over lay Canton Alley. Lillian always entered from Pender Street, through the great iron gate that led under the seven-storey apartment block. A courtyard opened behind, flanked by buildings rising along both sides. This was her favourite place in all Chinatown, because it felt like a walled fortress.

She reached the Wo Lun clothes factory and went in. To her surprise, the machines stood idle, just like the ones at home. The workers were playing cards at the back. A cloud of smoke rose from their cigarettes and conversation. One fellow looked up and gestured towards a curtain. "The boss? Old Mah's back there."

Lillian went up and rapped on the wall. She lifted the curtain.

"Elder Uncle?" she called out.

"Hmmm?" Old Mah turned from his desk and glanced up. There were newspapers, ledgers and ink brushes piled on the table, as well as dishes, chopsticks and spoons. A wooden bed stood to one side. Hooks and nails in the wall held his shirts, sweaters and pants. He smiled broadly when he saw Lillian. "Come in, come in. Don't mind the mess. Sit down by the fire."

There weren't many children or women living in Chinatown because of the travel costs and the special head tax that Chinese immigrants had to pay when they came into Canada. Like many men, Old Mah had come to Canada alone to work, and he fully expected to go home one day to his wife and children.

"Now, what brings you here?" Old Mah asked warmly. "You're Ho Jin Chong's daughter, aren't you?"

Lillian nodded. "Uncle, do you have any hand-sewing work? I could take it home and we could finish it in an instant! Anything you want sewn, we can do it. Buttons, button-holes, feather-stitching, hems, butterfly buttons, pig-snouts — we can do all these!"

Old Mah sighed and leaned back. He rubbed his shaven forehead wearily and fiddled with a pigtail neatly coiled atop his head.

"There's no work to be had. My men stay here just for the heat."

Lillian swallowed her disappointment. "Sorry to have disturbed you."

"Oh, not at all, not at all. Please give my greetings to your mother. If a job comes up, I'll send it over!"

Outside, she frowned. How could she go home?

Mama would laugh in her face.

She trudged wearily back towards Pender Street. Night had fallen over the city and Lillian felt pangs of hunger kick again. Money was the only thing that would keep them in Canada. Tomorrow she would go to more stores. She wouldn't quit until she found work! She wasn't going to China! It was filled with idiot men like Third Uncle. It was where they chopped off people's hands for stealing a few grains of rice.

She turned the corner and sprang back immediately. Just a short distance away, Third Uncle stood at the door of the Peking Restaurant, surrounded by four men.

"We'll eat our full and drink till we're drunk!" she heard him bluster loudly. "It's my treat tonight!"

"Sounds good, Old Ho, but can you pay?" called out a voice. "Your elder brother's not giving you money these days!"

"It would be different if you'd won tonight," added someone else. "But you've been beaten at the game-tables all day!"

"You're the expert at losing money!"

"Never mind my brother," muttered Third Uncle. "I've got money!" He rummaged in his pocket. "See?"

His friends whistled appreciatively. "What did you do? Sell the store?"

Third Uncle laughed. "I have my ways! I've got lots more, too! Let's go!" And he led the way into the noisy, steamy restaurant.

Lillian's forehead creased. How had Third Uncle got

his hands on so much money? Had he stolen it? Wait until she told Mama! They could report him to the police and have him arrested and taken away. That happy thought sent her skipping home.

But when Lillian came up to the darkened storefront, she suddenly remembered her own problems. Having Third Uncle arrested wouldn't stop Mama from taking them all to China.

An angry frown tightened her face, and she let out a long steamy breath. Then her thoughts buzzed. What if she could get some of Third Uncle's money? He said he had lots more! If she could find some and take it to Mama...

She sagged against the door. Mama would never touch stolen money. Then Lillian brightened. If she found Third Uncle's stolen money and hid it, she could tell him that if he wanted any of it back, he'd have to let Mama have some. He could tell her he had won it gambling.

Lillian took a deep breath, gripped the doorknob carefully and went in without a sound. The main floor lay dark because the boarders were still out at dinner. She knelt and unlaced her boots, taking a second to blow some warmth onto her fingers. Then she tiptoed towards the back of the shop, gingerly feeling her way along the work benches and tables. She heard the gurgle of the baby upstairs and the sounds of Mama moving about. She slipped by the puddle of light from the stairwell and into the back room.

She flicked the electric lightbulb on and waited to

"Returned, have you?" Mama looked up from her sewing with glittering eyes. "Did you find some more money? Have you finished running around?"

Lillian absently picked up a book.

"Leave your homework for now!" cried Mama. "Clear the table for dinner. It's late already. Blind-Eye will be up soon."

Lillian stacked her books and took them away to the girls' bedroom. Should she tell Mama about the stolen letter? Or about Third Uncle's money? When she linked the letter and the money together, an uneasy dread made her shiver.

She turned at the door. A single lightbulb threw a bowl of yellow warmth over Winnie and Nellie working at the sitting-room table. Mama was bent over, carefully brushing thread scraps into her palm. Maybe it was better not to say anything for now.

When she came back to the sitting room, she tried to act as if nothing had happened.

"No rice today?" she asked. There was just one pot steaming on the stove.

"Blind-Eye passed the bakery. Buns were selling cheap," answered Mama. "On a cold day people want food. Set the table and let's eat before Blind-Eye returns."

The steamed buns had been stuffed with meats or bean pastes. Nellie poured the tea, and the family sat down. After a few bites, Lillian cleared her

see if Mama noticed. Then she went quickly to Third Uncle's half of the bunk-bed. His stale-smelling pants and shirts hung over the wooden bedposts, and she rifled through the pockets. There were crusty handkerchiefs and dice and keys, but no money. She glanced furtively around, then knelt and dragged the suitcase from under the bed.

The fastener was rusty, but she forced it open. A foul stench burst forth and almost brought tears to her eyes. A bottle of liniment had cracked and soaked everything. Frantically, her hands travelled through the jumble of socks and shirts and underwear. Then her fingers stumbled over a suspicious bump in the bottom liner. Something was hidden there! Lillian poked around, and then groped under the cardboard.

It was an envelope! Slowly Lillian pulled it out and turned it over.

The letter was in Papa's handwriting, addressed to her!

3

FOR a long moment Lillian stared at Papa's handwriting on the envelope. She took a deep breath, and then another one. Slowly her trembling fingers pulled the letter out. It was dated September 7, 1909:

Dear Lillian,
Read this letter to your mother only when you are alone.

First, tell Mama that I am in good health. I hope she and the baby are both fine, too.

Attached to this letter is a ticket stub. Take it to the railway station counter for a package, before October ends. Inside the package is a very valuable notebook. Take good care of it until I return. Do not show it to anyone.

Tell your mother not to worry about me. Tell her that more people support my work now, but still it is not everyone. So I am very careful.

Tell Winnie and Nellie to obey Mama. I expect you to do the same and to work hard at school.

Along the margins, someone had pencilled in Chinese translations of Papa's words.

Lillian read and re-read the letter until the words were stamped into her mind. She held the letter to her face and sniffed for Papa's familiar smell. So! Three months ago, Papa had written to them. But where was he now? It was December, cold and icy through the province.

She refolded the letter and then looked carefully at the envelope. The postmark stamp read, "British Columbia." The ticket stub was noticed, so Third Uncle must have claimed the package. Swiftly she sorted through the suitcase but found no notebook. She knelt and peered under the bed, through the stinking shoes and slippers, but nothing. She lifted the thin cloth mattress and ran along the planks and notches but still came up empty-handed.

Third Uncle must have hidden it somewhere else! Lillian turned off the lamp and went upstairs. Her mind reeled. Third Uncle intercepted her letter and stole the package—that was how he had got his money! The notebook was valuable. Maybe there were money hidden in the pages. Or had Third Uncle sold off part of the notebook to make it so

"Mama," she started cautiously. "Why doesn't everyone support the revolution?"

Mama swallowed hard. Then she burst out, "Because some people value their lives, that's why! Because they respect the Empire, that's why! Because normal people aren't fools like your father!"

Winnie and Nellie stared down into their food.

"Doesn't Papa respect the Empire?" asked Lillian.

"Him? He wants to demolish the Empire!" Mama took a furious bite of bread and chewed angrily. Her eyes were fixed on some invisible point of air.

"But how?"

"None of your business!" cried Mama. "Children shouldn't be so nosy!"

"I'm not!" she protested. "I... I just want to find Papa."

"You? How? Run to the rooftop and shout his name?"

Fortunately at that moment Ruth began wailing. Mama took a final bite and left the table.

Lillian chewed doggedly on the bread and took a long swallow of tea. Why did she even bother trying to talk to Mama?

"Jeh-jeh?" Nellie called out "Elder Sister" in a quavering voice. "I don't want to go to China, not even after the baby's born."

"So? What do you want me to do about it?" Lillian's words lashed out like Mama's.

"You mean you'll go?" Winnie asked incredulously. "But in China cockroaches crawl through your bed!"

"People stand in the streets and sell children, especially girls," chimed in Nellie. "I don't want to go there!"

"Not even to learn to fly?" Lillian sneered. "You two are always practising roof-jumps like Blind-Eye's fighters!"

"Oh, shut up!" Winnie's face turned tomato-red. In the sword tales, knights and heroines leapt to the rooftops in a single bound. It was called "lightness power," and even Lillian had been intrigued by it. Once she had wondered whether running around all day with heavy weights attached to her feet would build enough strength so that she could fly through the air, too.

Footsteps sounded in the stairwell. "Oh, no! Here comes Blind-Eye already, " Nellie groaned.

Mama couldn't afford the Chinese school fees, but she still wanted her girls to be educated. So Blind-Eye taught them Chinese classics, reciting lines for them to memorize. The sisters hated the lessons, but on they plodded, with rhythm and rhyme keeping them going. On other days Blind-Eye gathered the neighbourhood children around him and told them stories. He might describe how the Great Wall of China was built with bricks and blood, or he could tell them about women disguised as men who joined the army.

The story-teller groped his way in, and Lillian quickly slipped over to him. "Blind-Eye," she said softly. "I know that Papa works for the revolution."

Blind-Eye's eyelids flickered imperceptibly. "Oh?"

"Mama told me so," said Lillian smoothly. "She said

you know Papa's plans for demolishing the Empire!"

Blind-Eye leaned back and thought for a while. "So you know all about the Empire, do you?"

"The Empire's the Manchus!" Lillian replied impatiently. "They're the northern tribes that conquered China four hundred years ago!"

"Their armies crashed through the Great Wall—" Nellie started.

"—and they made Chinese men wear pigtails to remind them of the conquest!" finished Winnie.

"That's right," nodded Blind-Eye. "China is starving now, and the people are angry about losing wars. But the Manchus don't care because they're not Chinese! That's why they won't spend money on modern education or western technology."

"Why don't they leave China?"

"Leave?" Blind-Eye laughed bitterly. "Why should they? They collect taxes and build themselves fancy palaces. They don't think of anything except how to keep themselves fat and in power!"

"So what will Papa do?"

"He wants the people to rise up and throw the Empire out of China!"

"But the Empire's still strong!" insisted Lillian. That was what the men in Stanley Park had said.

"No, it's not!" exclaimed Blind-Eye. "The Empire is weak now. It has been losing wars to England. Rebels are stirring the country. So the time is ripe for the final battle."

"Final battle?" her voice quivered.

Blind-Eye grunted. "When someone stands in front of the water tap and won't let you drink, even when you're dying of thirst, what do you do? Slink way and die? Or knock him down and live?"

* * * *

The next morning, Lillian did not want to wake up. She hugged herself tightly under the thick covers and refused to open her eyes.

She had dreamt that she and Papa were visiting Stanley Park once again, following the peacock around in the warm, shady trails. Shafts of sunlight pierced through the tall trees and curtained the air like nets. Lillian felt safe by his side.

Besides, Saturdays meant lots of hard work. In the morning she took the axe and went out back to chop a week's supply of kindling and firewood. All this, plus two pailfuls of coal, was carried upstairs and stacked neatly in the sitting room. Then the floors had to be swept and mopped. In the afternoon she emptied kettles of hot water into the great tin tub, and one after another the three sisters took their weekly baths. After the soiled clothes were scrubbed and hung to dry, sewing and homework were attended to.

By mid-morning she was already tired. Breakfast had consisted of two slices of bread and a mug of tea. All morning long she had re-lived yesterday's conversation with Blind-Eye. The revolution meant toppling the Empire, and the Empire was fighting back. Papa was one brave man who was not afraid! But what was he doing up in Revelstoke?

Lillian had to find Papa before it was too late. She had to tell him that Third Uncle had intercepted the letter and grabbed the notebook. He had threatened to sell the sewing machines and get rid of the business. The baby was coming soon and then Mama would take them to China. But the country was going to be at war!

The only person who could fix things was Papa. But he didn't even know what was happening at home! Lillian pulled out her school atlas and found Revelstoke. The town sat between two mountain ranges four hundred miles northeast of Vancouver. Her heart sagged. How could she ever reach Papa?

Lillian felt as if she was suffocating. What was Third Uncle up to? She had never trusted him. Could she have missed something in his suitcase in her hurry? How big could Papa's notebook be?

She dried her hands from the wash and took a broom into the deserted back room. The window at the rear let in some light. She looked about carefully and peered into every bed to make sure that no one was there. She swallowed hard, then knelt by Third Uncle's bed and reached under it for the piece of luggage.

But one of the metal buckles caught on the floor and the suitcase came out with a squeal. Lillian winced and quickly glanced behind her. She listened hard for a second, then bent over the rusty old clasp. It was jammed again, and she had to claw at it. Finally the lock gave way.

Suddenly a hand fell on her shoulder and seized her. Lillian's heart stopped. It was Third Uncle.

"Sneaky pest! What are you doing?" He thrust his face down to Lillian's and shook her. "I asked you a question, death girl!"

"I... I was sweeping the floor," she stammered, pointing to the broom propped by the bed. "Mama said to pull everything out from under the beds and to sweep it clean.... Someone was complaining about mice running around here!"

"Liar!" Third Uncle's tiny eyes bored into Lillian's face. The musty smell of tobacco poured out of his nostrils. Suddenly he released her and threw the suitcase open. The contents tumbled out and he ran his fingers over the cardboard liner until he felt the stolen letter. "If you come near my things again I'll whip you until you're limp, hear? You and your mother are under *my* say, do you hear that?"

"I was just sweeping the floor!" Lillian cried. "There's mice running around—"

Third Uncle's arm darted out and spun her around. For a man so slightly built, his strength surprised Lillian.

"Death girl, you listen good," he snarled, tightening his grip. "Don't get smart with me. You may know a few words of English, but you're not queen yet. I wouldn't hesitate to sell you or your sisters for five dollars a head! The women of this family are cursed with bad luck!"

Lillian gasped from the pain. Then she heard the front door.

"Mrs. Ho, are you there?" a woman called out.

Third Uncle sent Lillian stumbling out of the back room. She saw with relief that Mrs. Chang the Sunday school teacher had come.

"Oh, it's you, Ah-Lai," she smiled. "I have some good news for you and your mother. Is she at home?"

Third Uncle stomped through the two women and out the door without a word.

Lillian led Mrs. Chang to the stairwell, hoping that the teacher would not notice her trembling. Upstairs the visitor quickly passed over the polite formalities of adult conversation.

"We at the mission have been concerned about your family, Mrs. Ho," she stated firmly. "You can't feed four children when there's no money."

Mama stood rigid. Her eyes were glued to the floor.

"We think we can help, but the final decision is yours." Mrs. Chang nodded encouragingly at Lillian. "And you, Ah-Lai, are the key."

Lillian's eyes widened.

"A few days ago, the Bell family came to us," explained Mrs. Chang. "They're a nice Christian family, living in the West End close to the downtown. They have two little children ages five and six. They need a live-in housekeeper and maid. We immediately thought of you. They'll pay twenty dollars a month and Lillian will sleep and eat with them. I'm sure the Bells treat their servants well. So, will she go? And will you, Mrs. Ho, take her out of school?"

A job! Lillian's heart leapt. "Yes, I'm willing!" she replied quickly. A way to bring home some money! A chance to stay in Canada!

"Good," Mrs. Chang turned to Mama. "What about you, Mrs. Ho? What do you think?"

Mama paused for a very long time. "You and I know, Mrs. Chang, education is very important." She sighed. "But I'm carrying another body in mine. I've never felt so weak, not even when I had Ah-Lai and her sisters." Mama finally stared up with a pained look. "Ah-Lai will have to go to work. But just temporarily, until Jin returns, yes?"

Mrs. Chang nodded earnestly. "Oh, yes, just to help in the meantime." She turned to Lillian. "Will you come now? The Bells are at the mission, and I'll introduce you to start right away. They want help for Christmas!"

I'll be safe from Third Uncle, too, Lillian thought as they went downstairs. But what about Mama? What if he tries to sell Ruth?

Lillian and Mrs. Chang walked by the grocery importers, the jewellers and the barbershops that lined Pender Street. Crossing the railway tracks, they left Chinatown behind. On one side of the street were the stables where the meat packer kept his great wagons and horses. A blacksmith was next door and in the summer the children stood and watched the sparks fly from his forge as he hammered glowing pieces of iron into new shapes. But the cold had driven everyone inside, and all the doors were firmly shut.

"Mrs. Chang," Lillian burst out suddenly, "if Mama decides to go back to China after the baby is born, can I stay behind to work and wait for my papa to come back?"

The church matron drew back in astonishment. "My dear, you can't mean what you're saying! Your mother can't go back to China alone!"

Lillian looked away. After a guilty pause, she went on to another topic. "Mrs. Chang, who is Dr. Sun?"

"The leader of the revolution! And did you hear? He's coming to speak here! He's a Christian, did you know that?"

Lillian shook her head.

"Dr. Sun went to school in Hawaii and trained as a medical doctor," the older woman explained. "He travels to Chinatowns around the world, making speeches to rally support for his cause."

"But if he's the leader, why isn't he fighting in China?"

"Because the Empire would imprison him immediately. They kidnapped him in London a few years ago, but fortunately he escaped."

Kidnapped? Lillian wanted to ask more, but they had arrived at the mission. Reverend Chan introduced her to the church elders and then to a well-dressed couple. Mrs. Bell was delicate and thin with a peaked face peering from a collar of frilly lace. She smiled weakly at Lillian when they shook hands. Her husband wriggled his bushy sideburns and curled moustache. He grasped Lillian's hand vigorously and said with a grin, "I'm glad we've finally found some good reliable help!"

Lillian swallowed nervously and suddenly realized that she was about to start a whole new life. White people lived in a different world. They laid carpets on their floors and hung fancy paintings on the walls. Her school books showed pictures of grand staircases and glittering chandeliers in their homes. What was she going to do in their house?

"Lillian, the mission is pleased to help you," said Reverend Chan. "We've heard you are wondrously hard-working and reliable."

She gulped and nodded. But she didn't know how to bake pies or scramble eggs. What if she spilled the dinner and all the gravy onto a priceless carpet? And what if she dropped an expensive platter? Would she be fired? Or sent to jail if she couldn't pay for the damage?

Suddenly a loud rapping sounded at the door. A frantic-looking woman, bundled in furs and scarves, ploughed in like a storm.

"Pardon me, Reverend," she cried out. "But I must address the committee tonight!"

"What is it, Mrs. Carter?" Reverend Chan rose with concern.

"Two months ago," she started, "the mission in Revelstoke asked for our assistance."

Lillian's ears perked up. Revelstoke! That was where Papa's letter had come from!

"One of their Chinese members sent for his wife and child from China. He wanted someone here to look after them while he came down for them." She paused and sighed. "Unfortunately the man was killed in an avalanche. But the man's brother still wants the woman, Yiwen Mah, to go up to Revelstoke. He's sent the train fare down and all we have to do is find someone to take them up. But they have to go before the holidays. I have relatives coming at Christmas so I can't keep her any longer."

The Reverend pondered the matter. "Christmas is a busy time for everyone," he finally said. "I don't know anyone who could take them up now."

"Reverend Chan, I could go!"

Eyes all around the table swivelled to focus on Lillian.

"Could you?" Mrs. Carter ran eagerly over to her. "That would be splendid! You speak her language and would make a perfect travelling companion for her."

Reverend Chan held up his hand. "But the Bells need Lillian to help them through Christmas."

"Please don't worry," interjected Mr. Bell. "We can manage. It's more important that the young mother be cared for first."

Lillian's heart leapt. She was going to Revelstoke! She could find Papa!

* * * *

"Go where?" Mama demanded.

"Revelstoke. It's a town up north," answered Lillian quickly. Her hands toyed with the pins and threads scattered across the dresser-top. Mama was working in her bedroom tonight.

"Are they paying you?" Mama shook out the jacket she was hemming.

"No, I'm... I'm helping someone who needs a translator."

"*Helping* someone? You should help *this* family first!"

"But I am," insisted Lillian. "I can ask for news about Papa!"

"Oh?" Mama's eyebrow shot up. "You think he's there, do you? A thousand towns exist in this province, and you think you've picked the right one?"

"How would I know? I just want to try!" Lillian couldn't tell her about the stolen letter yet. If Mama confronted Third Uncle, who knew what he might do to her? Lillian herself had been surprised by the ferocity of his grip. But if she could find Papa and tell him everything, he would come home right away and deal with Third Uncle and the store's business. Then Mama wouldn't have to worry about a thing.

"You just want to take a trip for fun!" accused Mama, as she bit off the thread. "A tour of the countryside, that's what you want, isn't it?"

"No!" cried Lillian as her cheeks reddened. "I want to find Papa!"

"You can't go!"

"But the Bells said that I could go!"

"Are they your mother? I said no!"

"Why not?"

"You're too young to travel!"

"But old enough to work?"

Mama's needle halted in mid-air. Suddenly she looked so tired and grey. Lillian bit her lip and looked out the bedroom window.

"Ah-Lai, it's for your own good that I say no," Mama's voice dropped softly. "Do you know what the world is like out there?"

Lillian lowered her head.

"It's not very pretty. You're a girl, you're Chinese, do you know that?" Mama's voice rose dramatically. "People hate the Chinese. Men, they use women."

"But—"

"Hear me out! Chinatown here is safe. There's lots of Chinese here. Once you go off, it's hard to find a friend or a helping hand. And in the mountains there are wild animals and deep forests."

"But Revelstoke is a town, not a forest. There'll be Chinese there to help me!"

"Ah-Lai, I want Papa to come home, too." Mama's eyes shone earnestly. "But I can't lose another body from this family."

That was final, Lillian knew. When Mama played both hard and soft and still refused, there was no hope.

Lillian dragged herself into the sitting room, where Winnie and Nellie sat at the table doing their homework. They glanced up anxiously and resumed studying without a word. Lillian flipped open a book, but after a while she slammed the cover down and threw it away with a crash. She flung herself into a chair and thrust her feet onto the table.

"Don't let Mama see your feet up there," cautioned Nellie.

Lillian dropped her boots and twisted away furiously.

"Blind-Eye's coming up soon," Winnie chirped up. "Did you memorize the lesson yet?"

"No!" snapped Lillian, stomping towards the bedroom. "Just leave me alone!"

She fumed as she hurled herself onto her bed. She could have gone to Revelstoke! Maybe Papa was still there. Her mother was so pigheaded! She didn't know how dangerous Third Uncle could be. Lillian winced as she touched the bruise on her arm.

Through the open door she heard Blind-Eye's footsteps on the stairs. Then she heard Mama join him and the girls in the sitting room.

"Last night, what did we learn?" started Blind-Eye.

"Yang Family Woman Warriors," answered Nellie eagerly. This lesson was a hundred times more exciting than proverbs on how to become healthy, wealthy and wise.

Lillian closed her eyes and listened to her own angry breathing.

"You start then," Blind-Eye instructed Nellie, and she began reciting while he tapped out a beat on the table.

The family Yang possessed many sons,
Warrior men, brave and strong.
They led long armies to stem invasion
And gave their lives, for king and nation.

The wives assembled and raised an army
Of widow soldiers and women battalions.
They honed their spears, galloped their stallions
And marched for the frontier, the Yang House
    women.

Lillian buried her face in her pillow. All those flying
fighters and poisonous darts were nothing but fairy
tales! If China was really like the stories, then it
wouldn't need a revolution. And Papa would still be at
home. All those stupid Chinese people from China —
all they did was pass on lies. All they did was day-
dream and make trouble for everyone!

But even the pillow couldn't stop the lesson from
reaching her ears. In spite of herself, Lillian gradually
fell into the lesson's rhythmic story-line.

One boy walked tall, the only son,
But his mother decreed, the general was she,
"Too young to fight, you'll stay behind!"
To carry the name for the family line.

The boy's mother sounded just like Mama, Lillian
thought drowsily. She listened for the rest of the story.

But he was eager and he was keen,
Before the troops, he challenged her rule,

"You and I, we'll fight a duel!
Only if I lose will I stay home!"

Their blades engaged, sparks were dispatched,
They thrust and parried, their strength was
   matched.
The mother gained the upper hand,
Victory was hers, better than planned.
Then she saw fire in her son's bright eyes
And let him win, to join their lines.

Before the next stanza could start, Lillian had bolted
into the sitting room.

"I'm going, Mama!" she cried. "I'll run away and go
on my own! You can't stop me, Mama! Please don't say
no!"

"Crazy! Have you gone crazy?" demanded Mama.
She peered into her daughter's rigid face.

Lillian whipped her pigtails from side to side and
clenched her fists. "No, I'm not crazy! I have to go!"

"Have you ever heard anything like this?" Mama
turned to Blind-Eye, but he did not utter a sound.

"I'm not a baby!" Lillian said fiercely. "I'm going!"

Mama sat down and picked up her basket of mend-
ing. She held it to the light, sifting through the jumble
of cloth-ends and yarn as she searched for a needle.
Lillian held her breath and waited as her mother carefully threaded the needle. Finally Mama looked up.
"So you're like the Yang Family youngster, are you?
You're determined to go, is that it?"

Lillian nodded.

"Go then, go!" Mama threw her hands up in despair. "You're getting too big for your own good!"

Lillian stared at her mother, her eyes wide. Winnie and Nellie turned to one another in amazement.

"Take your woollen underwear!" Mama commanded.

"I know, I know." Lillian was still shaking. Her mother was really letting her go! To take a train, to travel far away on her first trip!

"In Revelstoke, there's one person to look for," Blind-Eye suddenly announced in a quiet voice. Lillian turned around. She had forgotten all about him. "A man called Ga-Lah-Boo Wing."

"Cariboo Wing?" she repeated. "Who's he?"

"Some say he's a madman, others call him a genius," said Blind-Eye. "He has his own mind, that's for sure."

"But who is he?" Lillian pressed. "And how do I find him?"

"Won't be easy. He lives alone, deep in the forests."

"Is he a hunter? Maybe he can hunt Papa down for us!"

"He's a hunter, and he's many things." A smile spread over the story-teller's face. "He's best known as a healer."

"But who *is* he?" Lillian demanded impatiently. "Did Papa know him?"

The old man shrugged. "They're the same kind of men, your papa and him. Dreamers! Men not afraid to walk alone."

"Wei!" A voice called from the stairwell. "Wei, Blind-Eye, it's your turn to wash now!"

He rose to his feet. "I'm coming now!"

"But what about Cariboo Wing?" protested Lillian. "You haven't told me—"

"There's nothing more," the blind man said gruffly as he groped his way by. "Go find him. He can tell you everything!"

4

AT Vancouver's dockside train station, the locomotive's steam whistle shrilled long and loud. This was followed by a mechanical shudder that rumbled and clanked through the chain of cars. At these warnings, the crowds on the train platform swept into an excited flurry of waving and noisy hugs.

Mrs. Chang peered anxiously at the billowing clouds of steam and cried out, "Hurry! Get on the train. Yiwen's waiting for you!"

Lillian nodded and swallowed. Then she looked hard at her mother. "Bye, Mama," she croaked out.

"Be careful you don't make trouble, hear?" her mother replied flatly.

For a long moment, Lillian searched her mother's face, but there was no expression there. Finally she seized Mama's hand and whispered urgently, "Be careful of Third Uncle!"

Mama shook her loose. "I'm not afraid of him!" she declared. "Get on the train!"

Mrs. Chang nodded and Lillian lifted her bag aboard. With a jolt the train heaved to a start and quickly left the platform behind.

Inside the railway car a young Chinese woman was waving at her, and Lillian stumbled into the seat beside Yiwen. Quickly she shut her eyes and prayed silently. What if something happened to Mama? What if Third Uncle sent them off to China while she was away? What if she didn't find any news of Papa and the trip was a complete waste? Maybe her mother had been right. Maybe this was foolish.

After a while, Lillian opened her eyes. Yiwen and her baby were looking anxiously at her. She was a big, hearty girl, with thick shoulders and strong hands. She looked older than fifteen, but her eyes sparkled wide and innocent.

Yiwen was awfully young to be a wife and mother, Lillian thought. But that was how they did things in China. Girls were married off early to get them out of their parents' house. She shuddered as she pictured what her own life would be like if she had been born in China. Maybe she would be married and carrying a baby around, too. Or maybe she would be tramping through the paddy fields pulling an ox and plough behind her.

"Not sick, are you?" Yiwen inquired. She spoke a rural dialect of Cantonese.

Lillian shook her head. "No, I was just finishing my

goodbyes." They looked out the window at the great ships in the harbour. Steam poured from the towering funnels of the Empress liners while the tall masts of the older sailing ships hung bare and silent.

"This harbour is beautiful," commented Yiwen. "Tall mountains standing next to the water. It reminds me of Hong Kong."

Suddenly the door to the car jerked open, and an unhappy-looking family of five stumbled forward, laden with suitcases and travelling bags.

"I warned you to be on time," the mother cried above her baby's wailing. "I told you we should have come earlier."

The harried husband peered about for vacant seats.

"Now look!" she cried. "We have to sit in a car full of Chinamen!"

Lillian stiffened. When she saw them coming towards her, she scrambled to move her bags away.

"Sit there!" the mother ordered the two children, pointing to the empty bench facing Lillian and Yiwen. "You, too!" she told her husband as she took the seat behind Lillian. "I'll lay the baby down here."

Lillian breathed with relief. At least she wouldn't have to sit facing that witch!

The husband gazed morosely out the window while the children stared wide-eyed at Yiwen and Lillian.

"Take off your coats!" barked the mother, and the children's hands jumped. But their eyes stayed glued on the two girls.

Yiwen placed her baby in Lillian's arms and pulled

a bundle from her bag. "Here, hold Wei-man for a minute," she whispered. "The restroom, where is it?"

Lillian pointed to the head of the car.

Yiwen strode down the aisle against the rolling and pitching of the train. The speed had increased now and the clickety-clack churned into a steady throb. Lillian saw many heads look up as Yiwen went by. A Chinese woman travelling on the trains was a rare sight indeed.

More than half the car's occupants were Chinese men. Clouds of smoke and laughter burst from one end where they were clustered around the stove. From their noisy jokes and loud chortles, they sounded like excited schoolboys going camping. Their rumpled suits looked as if they'd been slept in all week.

Lillian scanned their faces to see if Papa might be among them. Then she wished they would hush themselves before the white people started to complain. Why couldn't the Chinese read or smoke quietly like the whites were doing? Why couldn't the Chinese hold regular conversations in low voices?

Then Lillian glanced up and gasped. Yiwen had put on a Chinese smock, baggy pants and soft black slippers. She looked like a peasant woman or a servant girl. The heads of the passengers turned again to follow her as she went by.

"Ah, now I'm comfortable!" she exulted as she dropped her skirt and boots into a heap. "They tied everything so tightly that I couldn't breathe!"

Lillian groaned. "What did you change your clothes

for?"

"They were too tight! Mrs. Carter wouldn't let me wear anything Chinese. As soon as I came off the boat, she threw corsets and pantaloons on me and laced me up like a *joong* dumpling!"

"But this is Canada! You should dress like a Canadian."

"Even if it hurts your back?" Yiwen looked astounded. "You should wear whatever feels comfortable, that's what I say!"

"But it's different here," Lillian argued. The two children across from them stared like little owls. "We can't do everything we want. We can't upset the whites."

"But how will dressing like them make things better?"

Lillian cursed silently and wished that she could move to a seat at the other end of the train. She turned towards the window and watched the trees and telegraph poles dash madly by.

The door of the car opened again, and a voice called out, "Tickets, please! Please have your tickets ready!"

It was the train conductor, looking grave and serious in his uniform and peaked cap. Then he called out, "*Cheh-pew, m'goy. Cheh-pew, m'goy!*"

He spoke Chinese! Even Yiwen understood the badly mispronounced words.

"I didn't know the whites spoke Chinese," she blurted out.

"I guess on the trains it's different," Lillian finally

admitted. "The Chinese built the railway, you know." She went back to gazing out the window.

"They said my husband was clearing snow off the railway when the avalanche rolled down and buried him," Yiwen said softly.

They sat in silence for a while. Lillian massaged the bruise that still ached on her arm. What had Third Uncle done with the stolen notebook? If he had so much money, why didn't he give some to Mama? He was so anxious to sell the store and get rid of them all. Why did he hate them so much?

Suddenly Yiwen spoke up. "You don't like me, do you?"

"What?" Lillian floundered for words. "I don't know what you... I... I don't dislike you...."

"You don't like people from China, is that it?"

Lillian shrugged.

"Do you know much about China?" Yiwen asked.

"Sure, I know about China!" Lillian replied heatedly. "It's poor and dirty, so people move to Canada. China's always losing wars. Fathers sell their children for money. The women bind their feet up into stumps and can't even walk!"

"But those are only the bad things," protested Yiwen. "Don't you know any good things?"

Lillian turned away and looked out the window. She didn't want to talk about China. She didn't want anything to do with China. She just wanted to be left alone.

The train had left the city far behind and was passing through pastures and fields now. Snow had fallen and the shimmering expanses of white blinded her. If only she could find Papa and bring him home, everything would be all right.

Lillian's eyes soon wearied from the unending rush of scenery, and her head began to nod. She caught herself, and then saw Yiwen and her baby sleeping soundly. It must be tiring to be a widow so young. Had she cried much over losing her husband? A few minutes later Lillian, too, had dozed off.

She awoke to the sweet smell of steaming rice. She heard voices speaking Chinese. Yiwen was down at the end of the car chatting with the other travellers. The men chuckled as they told her how much they missed China. Lillian gritted her teeth. If they thought China was so wonderful, why didn't they go back? She had often heard the boarders in the store rave about the old country, where fruits ripened sweeter, meats tasted fresher and people were more honest!

Yiwen came hurrying back. Wei-man slept soundly on her back. "Ah-Lai, you've awoken just in time! We're making soup and rice," she announced excitedly. "Those men are really smart. They bought new pots, so they're testing them. They're railway workers! They bought provisions, too, so there's sausages and spiced bean curd. Come eat, while it's hot!"

"I'm not hungry," Lillian muttered.

"Not hungry? How can that be? You haven't eaten all day!"

"I said I'm not hungry!" she snapped.

Shrugging, Yiwen backed off. Meanwhile, the

mother behind was handing out cold potatoes and hard-boiled eggs to her family. Lillian pulled out her satchel. For dinner Mama had wrapped Chinese buns, crackers and slices of cold pork. Lillian nibbled at the dry crusts and stared out the window.

Bursts of laughter erupted at the stove where the Chinese had gathered. Everyone was urging everyone else to eat more and not to be shy about it. They were having a contest to see who could eat the most bowls of rice. Lillian's stomach growled. Something hot to drink would be nice.

"I wish they'd quiet down," sniffed the mother. "You'd think this was a Chinese restaurant!"

"At least they planned ahead for hot food," retorted her husband. "You call this dinner?" He threw a cold potato down in disgust.

"Go stick your fingers in their rice pot then!" cried the wife. "See if I care!"

That was the last straw! Lillian leapt up and marched loudly to the stove.

Yiwen smiled warmly at her. "Here, the soup is still hot." Lillian sipped it gratefully, and the heat rushed straight to her toes. The strips of ginger were fragrant, and she crunched on the almonds floating about. A spasm shook her. She hadn't realized how cold she was.

"Where're you going, girl?" An older man came up for the last of the soup.

"Revelstoke, Uncle. I'm going to Revelstoke," answered Lillian.

"That's a long way to go," he commented. "And in winter it's very cold!"

"I'm escorting someone there," she explained. "Someone who just arrived in Canada and can't speak any English." Then she added, "And I'm looking for someone, too!"

"Oh?" The man cocked an eyebrow. "What's his name?"

"Ho Jin Chong. Do you know him?"

The traveller pondered the name but shook his head. "Chinese people travel up and down this line all the time. Who can keep track of a single man? Who is he?"

"Oh... he... he's the father of a friend," she stammered. "The friend asked me to find him."

Lillian hurried back to her seat. She felt a flush of shame swirl on her face. She was afraid strangers would laugh at her story and call her stupid. They would think Papa an even greater fool. Suddenly the search for Papa loomed immense, like the great dark night outside. The train was taking her hundreds of miles into the wilderness to look for one man. How could she really find him?

After a while, Yiwen came back with Wei-man and sat down. "Do you want some rice?" she asked. "There's plenty left over."

Lillian shook her head. "Yiwen, your brother-in-law in Revelstoke, what does he do?"

"He works in a laundry."

"Has he lived there long? Does he know the town well?"

for him. Be careful, hear?"

shoved some wrinkled bills into her hand and backed off.

it!" Lillian struggled to turn and ask who he was what he knew. But the train had stopped, and was no time left. She found herself swiftly pro- out and down the steep steps.

odbye! And thank you again!" Yiwen shouted ily.

atch out for yourself!" replied the crewmen.

odbye, and thank you," echoed Lillian. She ed from foot to foot, trying to peer into the train. he couldn't see the man anywhere. Then it was all te, as the two girls stood on the platform and the lights of the train flashed by.

ian stood still to adjust to the un-moving land and ht about the strange man. Why had he waited he very last minute to approach her? Why had he er to be careful?

last car in the train finally passed and the two saw the lights of the town glowing from across ils. They picked up their bags and started walk- cross the steel tracks. Behind them loomed the utline of a great hill. Lillian suddenly wished as back on the train. No one else had got off in toke. The platform was empty.

en noticed Lillian's steadily slowing footsteps. ' She held out Wei-man. "You carry him and e the bags. It's easier if I carry one on each side ance."

"He's been there over ten years, I think," replied Yiwen. "Why do you ask?"

"It's... it's my father," faltered Lillian. "He's been away for several months and ... and we're getting very worried." Then, in a low whisper, she told her everything.

"Ah-Lai," Yiwen breathed. "Your father is very brave! In China, when rebels are caught, they're exe- cuted right away!"

Lillian's chest tightened. "I heard the Empire tried to kidnap Dr. Sun in London," she confided.

"What if they kidnapped your father, too?"

"My papa didn't tell anyone where he was going," Lillian said firmly. "They'd never track him down."

"But the Empire buys information, Ah-Lai. They can be ruthless!"

"So someone might tell them where Papa was for money?"

Yiwen shrugged as an unhappy look filled her eyes.

* * * *

The next day the travelling slowed. Time and again the locomotive pulled onto side tracks to allow freight trains to pass. In the morning they stopped at Kam- loops, where the bad-tempered mother and her family disembarked. The white passengers wished each other "Merry Christmas" as they said goodbye, while the Chinese bade each other "Take care" and "Go safely."

The Chinese workers were quiet today. Most of them

dozed through the day as if yesterday's noise and games had exhausted them. The leftover rice was boiled into a thick soup for everyone. Lillian's back ached badly. Sleeping while sitting on a hard bench was not easy. And once the fire in the stove had died, the car became frigid. Yiwen sat hunched in the corner of her seat, staring thoughtfully out the window.

The train left the rolling lake country and swung into the mountains. The rail line curved around and around through a coiling valley. Lillian felt as if they were entering a maze of mountains that swallowed everything. The rock face came so close that she could have reached out and scraped her palms against it. The peaks towered high above. She had to tilt her head up to see them. Here the summits did not curl gently over the horizon, but cut jagged across the sky. On the slopes, trees stripped of their leaves stabbed at the heavens like a legion of toothpicks.

The weather shifted constantly. Clouds fled from west to east, while the sun peeked out briefly. Out here the heavens seemed vaster and deeper. Wisps of mist lingered on the mountain ridges. Snow lay everywhere in thick heavy drifts. A stream, and then a chain of small lakes, wound by the tracks.

So these were the mountains, Lillian marvelled. In Blind-Eye's adventure stories, the orphan girls and survivor sons always turned to the mountains. Across rope bridges and past misty cliffs they trekked to seek

out the martial art masters. Up
secluded clearings, they learned
endure pain. When they strode back
tain, their hearts beat soft and stron
there training fighters for the revolu

It was dark but not late when
reached Revelstoke. Yiwen put on her
again and laced up her boots. Lillia
blankets and packed their satchels. T
crew came over to say goodbye when t
girls preparing to leave.

"Thank you so much for the food
exclaimed Yiwen. "You men have goo

"Take care of yourself," the men urge
Chinese stores as soon as you step off
cross the tracks and walk straight tow
Then turn right and go down the hill
you'll find the Chinese."

"Don't worry," Yiwen assured then
take good care of me."

The men took turns holding baby
last time, and then it was time to lea

At the crowded doorway, Lillian su
one clutch at her arm.

"I hear you're with Ho Jin Cho
muttered.

With a startled lurch, she turned
the railway crew stood close behind
face into Lillian's ear and whispere

Gratefully Lillian exchanged the heavy satchel for Wei-man. Not only did he weigh less than the bag, but he also generated some welcome heat.

She heard footsteps crunching from behind, and quickly turned. Two young boys were coming along, probably heading home for dinner. She fell back to following Yiwen, who marched sturdily ahead. The older girl gripped the two bulging satchels firmly, and two small string-tied packages dangled from her wrists.

Lillian hugged Wei-man closer, and her thoughts wandered back to the sudden gift of money. Had the man waited to give her the money because he was scared of being seen?

The boys had come up from behind and passed her by. Suddenly they sprinted up with a hoot, ripped the packages from Yiwen's wrists and charged ahead into the night. But before Lillian could even shout, Yiwen had dropped the satchels to chase them. Lillian strained to see the fleeing shadows through the darkness. Her heart sank. The thieves were too far ahead and were running too fast to be caught.

Suddenly Yiwen took a flying leap and sprang through the air like a panther. As Lillian stopped in amazement, Yiwen crashed down on the boys.

5

LILLIAN blinked. Could Yiwen fly? Was she trained in the martial arts to dive and fly with superhuman strength? She dropped the bags and ran to Yiwen.

"How did you do that?" she cried. "You sky-jumped twenty feet to knock them over!"

Yiwen was brushing the snow and gravel off her skirts. The two looted packages lay crumpled on the ground, but the hoodlums had disappeared.

"What are you talking about?" Yiwen looked up with a puzzled frown. "Lucky for me those silly boys slipped on the ice! I ran up and they pushed me over!"

"But I saw you!" insisted Lillian. "I saw you fly! I saw you leap through the air!"

"Ah-Lai, what are you saying?" Yiwen peered into her agitated face with concern. "I can't fly! I'm a human being, not a bird! You've been dreaming. You're tired, that's all. Wait here. I'll go and pick things up."

"No, I'm not dreaming!" Lillian stamped her foot. "And I'm not tired!"

Yiwen just shook her head and went to fetch their belongings. It was no use arguing any further, so Lillian followed her into town without a word. Soon they found themselves on a street where the store signs were dimly seen to be written in Chinese. The travellers quickly located the laundry and were welcomed by Yook, Yiwen's brother-in-law. He lived right in the laundry with two other workers.

Lillian was surprised that Yook looked about Papa's age. She had assumed that he would be younger since his brother's bride was so young. Yook stood thick and solid, with hands enlarged and hardened from years of scrubbing clothes in bleach and detergents. He seemed genuinely glad to see Yiwen. At least he wasn't a woman-hater like Third Uncle, Lillian thought with relief.

Yook set out pairs of chopsticks and laid out plates of leftovers which he had quickly reheated. "Eat, eat!" he urged the girls, whose eyes had widened with hunger. But Lillian's questions couldn't wait.

"Uncle Yook, did a man called Ho Jin Chong come through Revelstoke lately?" she called out.

The laundryman shook his head.

"Are you sure?" Lillian's voice dropped. "I ... I'm sure he came through here!"

Yook thought for a long moment. "No, I'm certain," he finally said. "Who is it?"

"My father," Lillian whispered. She stared blankly

at the bowl of rice waiting for her. But Papa's envelope had been marked with Revelstoke's name!

"Ah-Lai says he's involved in the revolution!" interjected Yiwen.

Yook looked up sharply. "Is that true?"

Lillian nodded.

"You had better be careful, then."

Lillian's face crumpled, and then Yook softened. "All day I stand in the back of the laundry washing and scrubbing," he said. "I really don't see who comes or goes."

Lillian looked up hopefully.

"Tomorrow, run over and ask at Wing Chong, the big store," Yook told her. "Maybe they know there. And start eating!"

Lillian slowly pushed the hot rice into her mouth, and when the warmth filled her stomach, she thought, "Of course someone at the store will have seen Papa!"

Yook laid thick mats on the floor for the two girls to sleep on. The next day he would move Yiwen and her baby into a boarding house.

In the morning, Lillian mapped out her plans carefully. She had two whole days to find Papa, because the return ticket back to Vancouver was for the following evening at 6 p.m. First she would visit all the Chinese stores. After that, if necessary, she would track down Cariboo Wing. Then she pulled her coat on and stepped outside.

The town was tiny, with houses and cabins perched timidly on the edge of a wide river that winter had reduced to a shallow trickle. But it was the view across the river that took her breath away. Huge squat mountains rose there. One looked like a gigantic ivory Buddha, whose enormous belly and thick arms protruded heavy and solid. Revelstoke was encircled by tall mountains. Lillian had never seen them so close up before.

There wasn't really a Chinatown — just two Chinese stores, four laundries and a cook-house called the Shanghai Restaurant. Across the street from Yook's laundry stood several taverns, a hotel and more cabins. There was little traffic on the ice-encrusted road. Only once did a horse and wagon clatter by.

A man from one of the laundries loaded bales of folded sheets onto a cart that he tugged towards Upper Town. According to Yook, most of the Chinese in Revelstoke worked in the railway repair sheds and on the nearby tracks clearing away debris. Other Chinese were cooks and servants in restaurants and homes in the Upper Town, where white families lived in little houses with tidy gardens.

The morning air was brisk and cold. Lillian thrust her hands deep in her coat pockets and marched into the Wing Chong store. The man behind the counter yelped with delight. "Wah! A girl! Where did you come from?"

"Saltwater City," she told him, calling Vancouver by its Chinese name. "Uncle, a few months back, did a man called Ho Jin Chong pass through here?"

The man rolled Papa's name over his tongue but

shook his head. "Never heard of him."

An hour later, a puzzled Lillian returned to the laundry and sank into a corner. She had gone to every building in Chinatown, but no one had seen or heard of Papa. Yet Papa's letter had clearly been sent from Revelstoke. He had been here! So why didn't anyone know anything?

Yook came into the back to move Yiwen's bags to the boarding house.

"Uncle Yook, how do I find a man called Cariboo Wing?"

"You want Cariboo Wing?" Yook's mouth fell open. "I thought only the old-timers knew about him. Many people think he's crazy!"

"I don't care," Lillian said firmly. "My father may have seen him. How do I find him?"

Yook shook his head. "It won't be easy. Cariboo Wing lives deep in the forest in a cabin all by himself. It's a long way off. It's too far for a girl to walk."

"No, it's not!" Lillian cried. "I'm used to walking!"

"But there are wolves lurking in the bushes," Yook countered.

Lillian gulped. "I'm not afraid," she stated, sticking her chin up.

"And did you see the clouds moving in?" continued Yook. "There might be a snowstorm!"

She shook her head vigorously. "Please, Uncle Yook, let me go. It's my very last chance to find my father!"

Finally Yook let out a long breath. "All right. You're

a big girl now. You should know what you're doing. But don't say I didn't warn you!"

"Thank you, Uncle Yook!"

"Now listen carefully! You need to follow the river north, out of town and into the bush. You'll come to a little creek that joins in from the side, but you ignore it. When you get to the second creek that cuts in, then you turn off and follow it up. Cariboo Wing's cabin is the only one built along that stream."

Lillian repeated the instructions to herself. Yook scrutinized her travelling clothes and pulled out a pair of thick pants for her. He tied a pair of snowshoes to her back in case she needed them. Then he packed some food for her.

"If you meet any wolves," he advised her, "don't be afraid. They'll be more scared than you! And don't stop too often, otherwise you'll become chilled easily."

Soon Lillian found herself marching swiftly along the riverbank. The prospect of failure throbbed like a bad headache. What if she had to leave Revelstoke without any news of Papa? Mama would laugh when she got home! And then there would be no choice. They would all have to go to China.

Gradually the town fell far behind. Packed snow covered the riverbank where the brush and trees sagged, but the water trickling down the riverbed thawed the ice there. All Lillian could hear were her own footsteps and the panting of her breath. She knelt to touch the tracks left by wild animals drinking at the river. Had they been left by bears? Or by deer?

Then the skies growled menacingly. Lillian glanced up and hurried on her way.

After a while her legs began to ache and her feet swelled tight inside her boots. But she refused to slow down. Maybe this was the price she had to pay to get Papa back. Maybe the gods were testing her, to see if she deserved Papa. Well, she would show them. She would walk all day and all night if she had to. She would become a warrior like — Yiwen?

The memory returned like a sharp smell. When she had mentioned the incident again to Yiwen that morning, the young mother had just smiled and shaken her head.

"It was dark, and you were tired. You've heard too many sword stories. Do you really believe people can fly through the air like panthers?"

Lillian had been taken aback. "Well...yes. Don't you think so? I mean, in China, a long time ago, they could have, couldn't they? Of course, they had to train and practise a lot!"

If Yiwen was heading out to Cariboo Wing's cabin, would she have to tramp through the snow like this? Or would she just spring from boulder to boulder like a flying tiger? Lillian sighed. Thoughts of flying always warmed her. Maybe Yiwen was a woman warrior in disguise!

An hour and a half later, she reached the second creek. Immediately it began to slope uphill. The creek ran narrow and steep, so the bushes closed in and tugged at her. Dead trees blocked the waterway, forcing Lillian to climb and crawl. And when she paused to rest, the stirring noises of the forest pressed in close and loud.

Then the need to take a pee became unbearable, and Lillian crashed into the woods to loosen her belt. She remembered to murmur, "Please, Uncles, step aside," so that any spirits hovering around would not be spattered upon. She glanced about fearfully. Were there wolves sniffing around? Quickly she picked up a stick, just in case she needed to fight back.

Surely she should have reached the cabin by now! Had Yook said to follow the second creek? Or was it the third? Lillian saw dark forests yawning endlessly before her. Worry gnawed in her stomach and aggravated the cold and hunger.

She had completely lost track of time and distance when she finally burst into a clearing. There stood a small cabin made of rough-hewn logs and sheets of cedar bark. A great stack of firewood lay neatly sheltered from the rain and snow, and up from the L-shaped stovepipe drifted lazy coils of smoke.

Lillian heaved a sigh of relief. A surge of strength sent her running to the door. She beat her fists on the heavy planks. "Wei!" she called out. "Is anyone there?"

When there was no reply, she tugged at the door. She swallowed nervously. Would Cariboo Wing be a madman with long hair prickling out like a porcupine's quills? What if Cariboo Wing didn't like girls?

The hand-hewn planks of the door slanted inwards,

so pulling them open was like lifting a trapdoor. It thumped shut behind her, and she stepped cautiously onto a packed earthen floor. Immediately the thick aroma of boiling herbs filled her nose. She let her eyes adjust to the gloomy darkness.

Then she heard a painful moan at one end of the room. She moved warily towards a grey blanket curtain, one slow step after another. Then she pushed it aside.

A bony old man kneeling by a bed whirled around. His eyes flew open. "Get out!" he cried.

Lillian stared in shock at the bed. A great bearded man, half naked, scarred and filthy, writhed as sweat poured out of him. A poultice of moss and grass covered one bloody shoulder, and his arms scrabbled frantically at the sides of the bed.

"Get away!" snarled the old man. "Want to die?"

Lillian fled. In the main room, she caught her breath. Was that Cariboo Wing? The man who had ordered her out looked about seventy years old, but there was uncommon fire in his eyes and voice. He had to be the healer that Blind-Eye had mentioned.

Setting her snowshoes down, Lillian looked around carefully. The one-room cabin was tiny. A table of rough planks stood to one side, with two wooden crates beside it for chairs. A fire crackled in the small iron stove. Tools, a gleaming rifle and several pairs of snowshoes hung on the wall. She went over and sniffed at the animal hides stretched on frames. The wall-cracks between the logs were stuffed with mud, moss and even cloth rags.

But she could see no medicine drawers. Lillian took her coat off and wondered how Cariboo Wing could heal without a stock of Old World herbs. The herb shop in Vancouver had a high cabinet with hundreds of little drawers. Some of the healing plants could even be harvested locally.

Lillian sat down with an impatient grunt and waited. She peeked out through the single narrow window at the grey clouds rolling across the darkening skies. She chewed the tips of her braids. She picked at loose threads on Yook's pants and watched puddles form around her boots. What was Cariboo Wing doing to the sick man? Why was he taking so long?

A sudden scream of pain jolted her. Cariboo Wing came rushing out and Lillian jumped up to greet him. He moved swiftly to the stove, ladled out the herbal broth, and disappeared behind the blanket again. But he also handed her a steaming bowlful of soup from another pot.

Lillian sipped it gratefully as she sat against a box to stretch her legs out on the floor. She leaned back wearily. Every inch of her body cried out for rest. The hearty soup warmed her from the inside. Her head began to nod and slowly her body shifted downwards. Soon she was lying flat on her stomach with her head cradled between her arms. The last thing she remembered was reaching out to pull her coat over her legs. Then she fell into a deep sleep.

* * * *

It was dark all around, snug and warm. Someone was calling Lillian from far, far away, calling for her to get up, insisting that she awaken. But Lillian was high on a rooftop with Yiwen. They were crouched low, peeking into the iron-barred windows below. Lillian saw Papa's face and jerked forward. But Yiwen caught her and whispered, "Wait until the guards go by..."

Lillian moaned and burrowed into the furry blankets. "Please leave me alone," she murmured. "I've got to save Papa."

But the voice rose in urgency and a hand shook her. "Girl, are you awake yet? Girl, are you awake yet?"

Lillian rolled over and forced her eyes open. Dimly she saw Cariboo Wing hovering by, rubbing his hands and blowing into them as if they were chilled.

Her senses snapped into place and she sprang up. "Is something wrong? What's the matter?"

"I need your help," Cariboo said quietly. "I cannot heal this man by myself." He poured a bowl of hot broth at the stove. "Drink this. Then come with me."

She rose in a daze. How could she help? She wasn't a doctor!

"Help me move him to the floor," grunted Cariboo when she followed him to the back of the cabin. "We can't do anything up here."

Lillian shrank back. Earlier the patient had been sweating and tossing. Now he lay deathly still.

When they finally heaved the man into place, Cariboo looked at her with eyes that commanded her trust.

"We have to hurry," he said. "Just do what I do. Don't be afraid."

He shook his fingers loose and sat down Indian style, with Lillian facing him over the patient. His right hand slipped under his shirt. "Put your palm down, just above your belly-button. It should feel very warm.

"Let that hand stay," he continued. "And now breathe from there. When air comes in, your tummy lifts. When it goes out, your tummy flattens."

Lillian fumbled around and pushed her stomach into action.

"Don't breathe too hard! Let the air float through your nostrils as if it were a fragrance."

She obeyed and heard him murmur, "Good, good. Just relax. Now close your eyes. Leave the other hand on your thigh."

Lillian glanced guardedly at the old man, but already his eyes were shut. Her mind darted about. Maybe Cariboo Wing *was* crazy, just as some people said!

"It's better without sight," nudged Cariboo's voice. "Less interference with your mind. Don't be scared."

She let her eyelids drop but strained to catch every sound. All she could hear was their breathing, rising and falling steadily. The sound filled her head. She felt it move from deep within herself. She felt it whistle through her nose. If her mother could see her doing this...

"Now put your left hand on his stomach," Cariboo commanded gently. She hesitated, and he reached out to take her hand. Lillian flinched with surprise. His fingers burned like a stove-top iron!

"You are becoming warmer, too," he said as he placed her hand on the clammy flesh. "This kind of healing is called 'hay-gung.'"

Lillian knew that "hay" meant breath, while the other word came from "gung-fu," the martial arts. Did this combination mean breath-fighting? Or battling with air?

"The human body is centred at the diaphragm, where your right hand rests," Cariboo said. "Those muscles bring air in and out of our bodies, so energy is created there. Hay-gung harnesses that life-force and lets you direct it. You can heal yourself or use it on others."

Lillian looked down fearfully. The sick man lay stiff and still. His skin had turned greyish-green. She swallowed hard. He looked dead already.

She calmed down and tried to listen to their breathing again, but her mind kept wandering. Had Papa come to see Cariboo Wing? Maybe Papa had been sick or wounded. Then he would have needed help. Did Cariboo Wing know about the revolution and Papa's notebook? Why had the man on the train given her money?

Carefully she peeked over at Cariboo, who sat still and erect. Then she stole a glance at the patient's face, too.

"You don't have to look," the healer said softly, as if

he'd heard her eyelids lifting. "Just breathe in and out as I do."

Lillian concentrated. In and out. In and out. She counted her breaths until the numbers bored her. This was ridiculous. She was wasting precious time when she could be looking for Papa. She just wanted to ask Cariboo Wing a few questions.

She cleared her throat several times but didn't dare speak out. She couldn't move, as if she were under a spell. Her seat itched and then a strand of hair fell on her nose, tickling it mercilessly. She felt her body tense up.

"Just a little while longer," Cariboo whispered. "I know you think this strange, Jin's daughter."

Lillian's eyes flew open, but the old man restrained her. "Don't speak, just keep breathing. Yes, I know you. You have your father's face, do you know that?"

She almost nodded.

"You have the face of your uncle, too," he continued. "No, not your Third Uncle, for I hear he's totally different. No, I speak of your Second Uncle, the one I knew."

Second Uncle? Of course there had to be a brother between Papa and Third Uncle. But hadn't he stayed in China? Suddenly she trusted every word that Cariboo Wing said. Her back straightened and her breathing slowed.

"How do I know you?" Cariboo's words floated over hollowly. "Jin and your Second Uncle, me and my son, we four worked on the railway, digging tunnels through the rock. Of course, all this happened long before you were born, when your papa first came to Canada.

"One day, disaster struck. The mountain caved in. Your Second Uncle and my son didn't survive. Jin and I went separate ways. When he came up here in September, there was lots to talk about!"

There was silence for a while. Then Lillian felt the sick man's belly shudder.

"You are young and strong," Cariboo murmured. "And sometimes an old healer like me needs help."

Her eyes flashed open for a second to see the sick man drawing in painful gulps of air. A few minutes later Cariboo said, "It looks done now."

Lillian glanced down and saw the patient's eyes flicker. Her face glowed as she sprang up. She had helped to save a life! She felt energy surge through her like fire.

They heaved the sick man back to bed and Cariboo fed him soup, one spoonful at a time.

"When does your train leave?" he asked.

"Six o'clock tonight." Lillian felt as if she could fly back to Vancouver, like Yiwen, like a bird!

Cariboo glanced at a pocket watch he drew from his shirt. "There's time. We'll cook and eat quickly to let you go. Can you stoke up the fire and bring in some water? Then we'll cook some rice."

Lillian skipped out and gathered snow and wood. At last there was someone who could tell her everything, just like Blind-Eye had predicted!

Quickly she brought in two pailfuls of snow, and then she gathered an armload of wood. As she came in for the final time, she saw that Cariboo Wing had put rice on the stove and was slicing up melons he had pulled from his root cellar. He laid out a slab of salted meat and talked as he worked.

"I've kept you waiting long enough." He looked up with apologetic eyes. "You came a great distance. You must have a lot of questions."

"Do you know where my father is?" Lillian asked eagerly.

When Cariboo shook his head, the power of haygung drained out of Lillian. "But you said Papa came to see you."

This time the old healer nodded, and she added, "Didn't he say where he was going or when he was going home?"

"No. Jin always kept his travels secret."

"To keep the Empire from following?"

"To keep anyone from following!" exclaimed Cariboo. He pulled off a strip of fat. "Up here, dishonest men would kill easily for his money."

"What money? Papa didn't have a lot of money."

The healer looked at her curiously. "Don't you know why he came up here?"

"To work on the revolution!"

"Doing what?"

She shrugged.

Cariboo washed the grease from his hands and wiped them dry. "Let's start from the beginning. Tell me, what is the revolution?"

"The plan to topple the Empire because they can't rule China properly," Lillian replied impatiently.

"And how do you topple an Empire that's four hundred years strong?"

"By getting the whole country to fight!"

"With what?"

"With...spears, I guess, and arrows and darts and axes?"

Cariboo laughed. "You've heard too many sword stories!" He reached into an earthenware jug and pulled out some ginger. Then he spoke seriously. "What the revolution needs are guns and ammunition and explosives. How else do you win a war?"

Lillian shivered. His words were filled with the sounds of death.

The old man scrubbed the ginger vigorously. "So you need money to buy the supplies. And that's what your father looks after. He goes to every town in the province, talking to people, asking for donations. And it takes a long time before people will listen to him and trust him."

So that's what the train money was for. "But Papa never sent us any money," Lillian told Cariboo. "He just sent a notebook."

"That's a hundred times more vital!" exclaimed the old man. "The notebook has the names of everyone who donated to the revolution. If it fell into the Empire's hands, many people here could die!"

"But if Papa was collecting money in Revelstoke,

why hadn't anyone in town seen him?" she demanded, fidgeting with the spoons on the table. "I asked in every store!"

"If you were travelling in secret, would you use your real name?" Cariboo lowered his voice. "This trip was a risky one because Dr. Sun needed money for the final big push. And now the Empire is fighting back. If the Empire can stop your father, it could slow down the revolution!"

There was a pause. "So Papa uses different names?"

Cariboo nodded as he sliced and chopped. Lillian felt stupid. But she also felt better. "Then no one could really follow him?"

"Don't worry. Your father's a very smart man. He carries a gun and he knows how to take care of himself."

Take care of himself! Mama had told the visitor from China that Papa just took care of himself...

Cariboo caught the wistful look on her face. "I guess things at home are not too good."

All the events of the past few days tumbled out of Lillian in a rush, and Cariboo sat down to listen. The only other sound in the cabin was the rice-pot lid clattering from the steam. When she finished, Cariboo shook his head sadly.

"I warned Jin," he sighed. "I told him a family man should stay out of the revolution! But he wouldn't listen. He kept saying he had to do it because he didn't want the whites looking down at his children." Cariboo Wing looked hard at Lillian. "Your father didn't want his children to grow up and hate being Chinese!"

Lillian blinked.

"And then he lectured me!" Cariboo went to the stove to start cooking. "Can you imagine? People come to beg for my help, and your papa stood there, telling me what to think! 'China is weak and backwards!' he shouted at me. 'It needs modern education and a modern army to win respect from the West! But the Empire won't change, so we have to force change!'"

An eerie feeling suddenly came over Lillian. She felt as if she and Papa were staring at each other and reading each other's mind. Papa had seen into his children's future! He wanted to change the world for them! He cared for them so much that he was willing to risk his life! She shut her eyes to let the news sink in.

When the hot dishes were brought over, Lillian began to eat. But she couldn't swallow, though she tried and tried.

"What's the matter?" Cariboo asked. "Don't you like my cooking?"

She set her chopsticks down and gripped her trembling hands. "No, the cooking's fine. It's...it's when I think of Papa now, I get so scared! People want to kill him — for his money, for his notebook. I hate the revolution!"

Cariboo stared intently at her. "Tell me, how did you know to come here?"

"Because of Papa's letter!"

"That's strange." Cariboo's forehead creased slightly. "I didn't think Jin would give such details away."

"He didn't!" exclaimed Lillian. "I read the postmark stamped on the envelope!"

"And there hasn't been a second letter?"

She shook her head.

"I thought there might be one," Cariboo said. "Jin would want to send money to your mother soon. He knows there are accounts to be settled before the year's end."

"Maybe Third Uncle took that letter, too!" she cried.

Cariboo sighed. "It's unfortunate how the revolution tore those two brothers apart."

"What do you mean?"

He peered at Lillian again. "Your parents don't let you know much, do they? Here, if you start swallowing your food, I'll explain everything. How about that?"

She nodded and picked up her bowl.

"To begin with, there were three brothers in your papa's family," he started. "Before Jin and your Second Uncle came to Canada, your grandfather divided his lands in China equally among them. Your Third Uncle was the youngest, so he stayed behind to farm the land, even though he yearned to come here. When Second Uncle was killed, he pleaded to come. But your grandfather said no. So Third Uncle stayed in China and thought that the third piece of land would be split between Jin and him.

"But your papa didn't do that. When your grandfather died, Jin sold Second Uncle's piece and used part of the money to bring Third Uncle over. The rest he gave to the revolution. I heard that Third Uncle shouted in the streets for days that your papa had cheated him!"

"But Third Uncle had his own piece of land," Lillian pointed out.

"He had lost it in a gambling match long before Second Uncle died," replied Cariboo. "And when he went to borrow money from Jin to get it back, your father refused. He had no money, anyway. Then Third Uncle's wife ran away in shame and the whole village laughed at him. So he blames your father for all his losses!"

"Then... then he wouldn't hesitate to sell Papa's notebook?"

"Not at all. He's a very dangerous man. Many times, he's even threatened to kill your papa!"

6

IT had started to rain again in Vancouver. Mrs. Chang forged ahead, clearing a pathway through the throngs of anxious people milling about in the railway station. Lillian followed close behind. The throbbing and rumbling from the trains, the hubbub of the crowds and the incessant press of bodies threatened to drown her. Lillian's body ached. After the hike back to Revelstoke from Cariboo Wing's cabin, she had sat on the train next to a fat pumpkin of a man who had snored all night like a sawmill. She hadn't slept a wink.

Still, the trip had infused her with new energy. Now she knew all about Papa and his involvement in the revolution. Now she understood why Papa had been so willing to leave his family behind and risk his life. But learning about Third Uncle's hatred of Papa had saddled her with new worries. Had Third Uncle stolen another letter? And did he know where Papa had gone?

Finally the two women made their way to the station entrance, and Mrs. Chang quickly led the way to a waiting horse and buggy. As they boarded, she announced, "I'm taking you straight to the Bells' now."

"Oh, no!" cried Lillian. "I have to go home first!"

"There's no time," ruled the church matron.

"But I have to—"

"Ah-Lai, listen to me!" Mrs. Chang cut in sharply. "There's no time to argue." She paused. "Your mother's very sick."

Lillian halted abruptly. "How—"

"Don't worry," the older woman hurried on in a kindly tone. "I have things under control. I visit her every day, and your sisters are staying with me. But your mother needs medicine and there's no money. You must start work right away and try your hardest to make a good impression. Then you can ask Mrs. Bell to pay a week of your wages ahead of time. Will you do that?"

Lillian nodded reluctantly. She didn't have much choice. But how could she do something about Third Uncle before it was too late?

Within minutes the carriage had pulled up in front of the Bells' house. Lillian stared at the castle-like turret and conical roof that dominated one end of the building. They stepped through the bushy hedge surrounding the yard and walked up the wide steps. The house was painted a deep green, with diamonds of red and yellow stained glass bordering its many windows.

Mrs. Chang knocked on the door, gaily decorated

with a wreath of holly, pine cones and red ribbons. Lillian clenched and unclenched her cold hands. When the door was answered, she saw flour threaded through Mrs. Bell's hair and patching her skirts in white clumps. Mrs. Chang whispered goodbye and squeezed Lillian's arm as the girl was quickly pulled inside.

"Oh, I'm so glad you've come!" her employer cried. "There's so much work to do for dinner tonight. I'm having the whole family over!"

Lillian glanced nervously around at the mirrors and fancy gilt frames hanging along the hallway. Even the wallpaper gleamed with golden strokes. She breathed deeply as Mrs. Bell took her coat away. The air hung thick and stuffy as she fought to concentrate on the situation at hand. She had to find money for Mama's medicine. Worrying about Third Uncle would have to come later. Maybe Mrs. Bell would send her to Chinatown on an errand, and she could slip into the backroom at home for just a second!

"You Chinese are the most hard-working people on the earth!" Mrs. Bell told her as she led the way into the kitchen. "We had to let our last girl go. She was the laziest thing I'd ever seen. After she was gone, I had to count all my silverware, piece by piece. You just can't trust those Irish!"

She held out a stiffly starched apron, and Lillian looked around. Her eyes almost popped. The sink overflowed with red and green apples, stalks of celery, and bunches of carrots and turnips ready for scrubbing and cutting. Three layer cakes sat on the counter waiting to be frosted. Greasy cake pans and blackened baking tins soaked in a tubful of water. On the long table by the window lay a huge ball of pastry dough and a stack of pie pans. It didn't look as if she would get to run out to Chinatown today. She sighed.

"Here, start peeling these!" Mrs. Bell led her to a huge sack of potatoes. "And watch me roll out the pastry so you can do it later."

As endless curls of brown skin coiled and slipped off her paring knife, Lillian thought about Third Uncle. If she could go through his belongings again and find a second letter, she might discover where Papa had travelled on to, and then she could tell Mama.

But Mama was sick now. She couldn't do anything about Third Uncle, no matter what they found out about him. Even Lillian couldn't do anything, trapped in this huge fort of a house!

"Are you paying attention?" Mrs. Bell crisply broke through Lillian's thoughts. "The dough has to be rolled very thin, do you see? And hurry along, will you? The silver is waiting to be polished."

The silverware was ornate, heavy and dull. Mrs. Bell, who was spinning from stove to counter to sink like a whirlwind, saw Lillian hesitate at the great number of pieces: two knives, two forks and two spoons for each of the sixteen settings, plus all the ladles and serving spoons.

"Better get started!" she called out.

Lillian brooded angrily as she heard her stomach

growl. She hadn't eaten all day! Her mouth watered as she watched Mrs. Bell baste a huge side of roasting beef. She listened to the happy whoops of the children prancing around in the parlour. There, a huge evergreen tree filled the house with a fresh sweet smell. Under a glittering silver star, coloured balls, bells and long garlands of gold bobbed and twinkled among the heavy branches.

When Papa came back she would tell him to throw Third Uncle out! The old weasel was probably running around drinking whisky with his no-good cronies while Mama lay sick in bed. And what had he sold to get his money? Was it the secret about Papa's location? Or was it the notebook?

But all she could do for the time being was to stand there and continue the polishing, one piece at a time. Then she had to wash and cut the vegetables, knead the dough for the dinner rolls, and spoon fruits and cream into the pastry shells.

In the dining room, bright paper streamers curled across the ceiling to meet over the glistening chandelier. Boughs of glossy holly and evergreen peeked from behind the mirrors, around the door and window frames, and even over the mantelpiece. As the guests arrived, the elegant lamps were flicked on, filling the house with rainbow shades and colours. The air thickened with laughter and cigar smoke.

When the table was set, Lillian donned a clean apron and carried the laden platters out to the candle-lit table. The glittering dishes flowed unendingly from the kitchen to the dining room and back. Over and over she warned herself not to spill a drop or let anyone know she was nervous.

She felt curious eyes linger on her and heard muffled giggles from the girls. They were not much older than she was, but they wore pretty dresses with puffed sleeves and lacy collars. Glancing down at her own faded dress, Lillian suddenly felt ashamed. Each trip into the dining room became a nightmare.

When the table was finally cleared and everyone had retired to the parlour for brandy and coffee in front of the fire, Lillian weakly surveyed the mountain of dirty dishes waiting for her. At least she hadn't broken any!

She was elbow deep in the greasy dishwater when Mrs. Bell danced gaily into the kitchen to fill the coffee pot.

"Oh, everything's turned out so well!" she gushed, weaving slightly with a glass of wine in her hand. "You Chinese are so well behaved! Wait until my neighbours see you! They've all got Chinese houseboys, but I'm the first to get a Chinese girl!

"Now, my girl, if there's anything you need, just let me know. I want to make your stay here as comfortable as possible. Don't be afraid to ask!"

"Well, yes," Lillian pounced on the invitation. "There is something, Mrs. Bell. Could . . . could I please have a week of my wages early? My mother, she needs some medicine . . ."

Mrs. Bell's smile vanished at once. "Isn't this a bit

sudden?" she asked coldly. "After all, you just started today. How do I know you'll stay a week?" With that, she turned and left with her coffee pot.

Lillian gulped and thrust her hands back into the soapy water. No money meant no medicine for Mama. Her illness couldn't be good for the baby inside her! If only Cariboo Wing were here, he could make her well again...

Quickly Lillian glanced at the clock. It was almost seven-thirty. She wiped the perspiration on her forehead and began scouring the pots with renewed strength.

When all the dishes were dried and put away, when the floor was swept and all the counters were wiped clean, Lillian stole cautiously into the parlour. Despite the blazing fireplace, this room felt cooler and more comfortable than the kitchen. Mrs. Bell was playing the piano with her guests clustered around laughing and singing Christmas carols at the top of their lungs. After waiting a while, Lillian drew Mr. Bell aside and told him that the kitchen was clean and that she was going to bed.

"Won't you join us?" Mr. Bell smiled congenially. "You can sing along with us!"

Lillian looked at him in disbelief. He nodded and offered her a platter of shortbread cookies. She looked longingly at the happy faces, the warm glow of the piano and the sweet-smelling Christmas tree. They were singing "Deck the Halls," her favourite carol.

"Don't be shy!" Mr. Bell encouraged her with a twinkle in his eyes. "Come along and I'll introduce you. We're all very nice people, you know."

"No, I...I can't!" Lillian stepped back and fumbled at her apron. "I...I'm really tired. I just got off the train this morning. Thank you, anyway...and good night!" She turned and fled from the room before she could change her mind. She had to see her mother.

* * * *

As she went running over the hill on Pender Street that led down to Chinatown, Lillian suddenly realized what a stupid thing she had done. What if Mrs. Bell discovered she was gone, and thought she had run away with the silverware? She might call Mrs. Chang. Or the police!

But it was too late to go back. She had arrived in familiar territory. Past the warehouse, the horse stables and the iron foundry. Past Uncle Woo's cafe. Across Canton Alley and Shanghai Alley. Then all of Chinatown's familiar storefronts and signs surrounded her. She felt her heart quicken and wondered how Mama would look. She couldn't remember her mother ever being sick.

Lillian turned the corner and was almost home when the door to Hing Kee opened. Out stepped Third Uncle, wrapped in a long coat. She stopped and stepped aside. It was the old weasel himself! But where was he going? Gambling? Drinking? Or out to sell the second letter? She stuck her head out and saw him heading the other way towards Columbia Street. Without a moment's hesitation, she pulled her hat down tight and followed.

She edged close to the darkened storefronts all along the street, ducking into doorways and hallways whenever possible. The low glow of the streetlamps helped conceal her presence. She prayed that he wouldn't suddenly spin around and check behind him. When he turned north, she ran as fast as she could to the corner.

There she stopped and peered gingerly around. Third Uncle was disappearing into the deeper darkness of Market Alley. This was the cluttered back lane between two streets, but even there the Chinese had struck a full set of storefronts. At night, only the restaurant doors threw out any light.

Lillian hugged herself tightly and hurried after him. The alley was momentarily deserted at the height of the dinner hour, and only Third Uncle moved through the darkness. He had lit a cigarette, and the pinprick of orange light signalled his movements. She carefully avoided the crates and garbage strewn all around. One clang or clatter, and Third Uncle would discover her! She heard her breathing come hard and fast.

Then the bobbing lantern of orange took a sudden dive and disappeared. Lillian marked the location as best she could and crept up swiftly.

From a dark doorway, Lillian heard voices murmuring. She groped her way cautiously towards the sound. She went as close as she dared and squatted down. Her breath seemed to wheeze in and out like a howling wind. She listened hard.

"...you're not going to go after Dr. Sun?" she heard Third Uncle demand.

The other voice laughed. "Why bother? His revolution is doomed! Besides, if I did something here, the white newspapers would make the Empire look bad."

"So my information was good?"

"Yes. We found your brother. The second letter led us straight to him."

So Papa *had* sent another letter! Lillian caught her breath. But what had this man done with Papa? Her heart began to race.

"So when is the rest of the money coming for the notebook?" Third Uncle asked cockily.

"I said I didn't know," answered the man. "I warned you your price was too high. That's why it's taking so long."

"Long?" sneered Third Uncle. "By the time you get the money, the revolution will be won and the Empire will have been toppled!"

"Shut up!" commanded the other voice fiercely. "The notebook isn't worth that much, you know."

"Hah!" Third Uncle laughed. "You've been waiting all these months to tell me that the Empire doesn't want the list of names? You even gave me an advance to make me promise the notebook to you! The Empire isn't afraid of Dr. Sun, is that right?"

There was a pause, and then Third Uncle's companion spoke up. "I could make you lower your price, you know."

"Oh? How?" Third Uncle exhaled confidently. "The Empire needs that notebook to stop the revolution. It's the money from the overseas supporters that gives the rebels all their guns and ammunition. You know that and I know that. And once the Empire knows who the donors here are, it can stop their donations by threatening their families in China. So let's stop playing games!"

"I could make you lower your price," the man repeated slowly. "How would you live if Chinatown knew all the facts?"

"What are you muttering about?" Third Uncle sounded impatient.

"What if people learned the truth?" continued the man. "What if people could see clearly that you had no heart? How long would you live if Chinatown knew that you'd killed Ho Jin Chong?"

7

KILLED Ho Jin Chong? Killed? Papa was dead?

Lillian stuffed her fist into her mouth. It couldn't be!

"Listen to me, fool!" snarled Third Uncle. "My brother died on me long ago. He's nothing to me. If my price drops, so does your profit. Remember, the more the Empire pays me, the more you'll get for being the middleman!"

Third Uncle let his words sink in. "Besides, I didn't kill my brother. I just told you where to find him, that's all."

"That's all?" the agent snorted. "You turn his death into a choice of words! Your brother's life was just dollars and cents to you, wasn't it?"

"Too bad you people couldn't track him down on your own," Third Uncle said coldly. "Now, what about the money for the notebook?"

"Your price is too high."

"Don't toy with me," snapped Third Uncle. "My price is fixed!"

Finally the agent spat out, "Have it your way, fool. It will take four weeks, maybe five before I can get an answer."

Third Uncle's voice was cool. "You make that two weeks. I'm not waiting forever. Don't forget, there are others who will pay for the notebook, too!"

The two plotters clomped off in separate directions, leaving Lillian huddled in the gloomy darkness. Their footsteps died away, and then the faint din from the nearby restaurants filled the alley.

Tears were streaming down her face when she finally pulled herself up. Papa was dead. He was gone. Her prayers hadn't worked, and her trip to Revelstoke had been useless. The good-luck peacock was nothing but a stupid superstition. Lillian's stomach churned and she bent over to retch. When the spasms stopped, she groped her way back to Pender Street. She had to get back to the Bells'. She couldn't face Mama now.

The cold and the tears stung her cheeks as Lillian trudged up over the hill. All she could see was Papa's face breaking into that smile of wonderment as they had watched the peacock open its fan. Both of them had been fooled by the bird and its beautiful feathers. Even Blind-Eye thought the peacock's fan brought good fortune. Instead, that was the day that everything had started going wrong.

Great racking sobs choked out of her. Chinese people thought that crying brought bad luck. But Lillian didn't care anymore.

As she drew near the Bell house, she swallowed and

tried to contain her tears. She couldn't let the Bells see her like this. She couldn't tell them about Papa. And she couldn't tell Mama, not until after the baby came. Mama was too sick to hear any bad news now. What if she should die, too? Lillian shuddered.

Then the thought of the unborn baby made Lillian cry all over again. It might have been a son! Papa would have taken him from store to store in Chinatown for show. He would have held the baby close to his face and whispered secrets to him.

When she had calmed down a bit, she sneaked in through the basement back door and ran quickly to her room. Kneeling by her little cot, she lay down her head, first to cry, and then to pray. She asked God for help and begged Gwoon-yum, the Goddess of Mercy, to look over and protect Mama.

The tears would not stop. She sat up, she went to the door, she curled up on her bed. But no matter where she went, the crying kept coming. Her head throbbed with pain, her stomach ached. Finally she crept into bed.

The next morning, Lillian practised smiling before heading upstairs. When she was busy stirring porridge and boiling eggs and making toast, she thought she would survive. But when she had to take the tray into the dining room, her arms felt like rags.

She walked into the dining room with the dishes clattering nervously on the tray. The children tugged noisily at the toys they had brought to the table, but Mr. and Mrs. Bell looked groggy and grey. The first platter of toast crashed into the cutlery and glasses as Lillian tried to keep the tray balanced in one hand. Absently, Mrs. Bell's eyes flickered, and she tried to smile. Lillian looked away from her. Mr. Bell's moustache twisted as he yawned.

"Good morning, Lillian," he called out. "Did you sleep well?" But she turned hurriedly away and almost ran back to the kitchen. How could they go on eating and talking when her papa was dead?

Mrs. Bell came in. "Are the eggs done yet?"

Lillian dashed away her tears and bent over the stove to hide her face. "I'll bring them out right away."

"Oh, Lillian." Her employer turned at the door. "Please smile. It's the holiday season, for heaven's sake!"

That night, when she turned out the light and slipped into her cold bed, Lillian's weeping renewed itself as if it had never started. What was she going to do? Why had Papa become involved in the stupid revolution in the first place? Now she was the only one who was crying for him. Maybe that was why it wouldn't stop.

The next morning, Lillian's stomach still ached, but her mind felt calmer. It was floors day, and she started right after breakfast. She gathered the rugs from throughout the house and hung them outside. Then every floor was swept and all the furniture dusted. After lunch she and Mrs. Bell rolled the larger carpets up and took them outside.

Lillian swung the carpet-beater into the rugs. The

dust flew up in clouds at each stroke. She was soon sweating in the cool winter air, but she hit every square inch of the carpets. Somehow the hard work took away part of the hurt.

"My, you're a strong girl!" Mrs. Bell marvelled. "Usually Mr. Bell does this job."

That night, Lillian pulled on a wool hat and thick socks to fight off the cold before getting into bed. She wondered if she should light sticks of incense or offer chicken and rice to comfort Papa's soul.

The next day, she bathed the children and scrubbed their clothes. She changed the bedsheets and watered the houseplants carefully. As she was slicing the bread for lunch, she thought of Third Uncle. He had killed her father. He was a cold-blooded murderer. Lillian stared at the bread knife gleaming in her hand. If she had the chance, she would show Third Uncle no mercy!

By the time her day off arrived on Sunday, Lillian was too exhausted to cry anymore. A week of hard work and little sleep and food had left her drained. There was nothing left for the Hos to do with their lives now but to get out of this country. As soon as the new baby was born, they would go back to China. In her pocket, Lillian clenched the dollar bills Mrs. Bell had given her for her pay.

The streets of Chinatown buzzed with activity as Lillian drew close to home. In Shanghai Alley, a crowd was jammed in front of the Chinese Theatre, waiting for the doors to open. Dr. Sun was speaking later in the afternoon. On Pender Street, men sauntered from the teahouses into pool halls and stores. Gwoon-fong the delivery man sailed by, balancing a trayful of hot dishes on his shoulder with one hand and steering his bicycle with the other. The doors of Chinatown were not garlanded with holly and ribbons like those of the West End. You would never know that the holiday season had arrived by looking around here.

Coming up to the family store, she saw men carrying sewing machines out of Hing Kee and loading them onto a wagon. Fat Old Wong stood there counting the pieces and watching every move with his beady eyes. Lillian halted in her tracks. Mama had sold the machines to get the money they needed to go to China.

After the wagon had pulled off, she walked slowly into the store. Her footsteps echoed in the empty room. The tables and benches had disappeared. The long wall cabinets stood naked and abandoned. The store looked as if it had been looted. Only the little altar to Gwan Gung, the patron god of war and merchants, had been left behind, probably because it sat high up on the wall. Faintly she heard the clatter of mah-jong tiles rise from Mrs. Kwan's game session next door.

She was heading up the stairwell when she heard Third Uncle's voice whip out from the back room.

"You, Blind-Eye, I thought you had left! Have you paid your rent yet?"

Lillian halted and heard the story-teller reply evenly, "No, I have nothing for rent. You know that."

"You think you can stay here forever?" shouted Third Uncle. "You're useless, do you know that? Now get out! We don't take in beggars!"

Lillian slipped down to the door and peered into the back room. Blind-Eye sat erect on a chair with his hands resting on his thighs. Third Uncle swayed unsteadily before him, a rolled-up newspaper in one hand, a cigarette in the other.

"Blind man, are you deaf, too?" Third Uncle leaned over and blew a mouthful of tobacco smoke into Blind-Eye's face. "I told you to get out!"

When Blind-Eye did not move, Third Uncle cursed furiously and swung the newspaper like a club down at him.

"No!" Lillian shouted. She ran into the room as Blind-Eye blocked the blow with one swift arm. It was as if he could see!

"Fool!" Third Uncle unleashed a flurry of oaths. Then he spotted Lillian behind him. "Death girl!" he sneered. "Returned, have you?"

She stared at him without a word.

"The death girl is back from her job," snickered Third Uncle. "She thinks work is like fun and games. Wait until China. Then you'll know what work is!"

He looked her up and down like a piece of furniture. "Girls in China are garbage, do you know that? Drop them down wells and sell them at the market. Right beside the pigs and geese! And they really work: slave girls, sing-song girls, girls who grind flour with stone mills, girls who go blind from embroidery!"

He crushed his cigarette underfoot, then turned and cackled all the way to the door. "She thinks she's lucky!

She has clothes to wear and food to eat. Wait until she's in China! Then she'll see!"

Lillian went up the stairs very slowly. Cariboo Wing was right. Third Uncle was a sick man. Sick and dangerous.

Mama was propped up in the iron-framed bed with heavy blankets over her legs and an old shawl on her shoulders. Her head lolled limply forward, and her hair hung in uncombed tatters. Lillian ran up in alarm. She had never seen her mother in such a condition.

"Mama?" She nudged the sleeping woman gently. "Mama, how do you feel?"

Mama's head lifted and her eyes pulled open painfully. "Oh," she murmured, "Ah-Lai, you've returned, have you?"

Lillian peered anxiously into the ashen face. Mama's eyes rolled aimlessly in the hollows above her sunken cheeks. Her breathing scraped out of a chest that was painfully congested. Lillian felt her own eyes smarting, but she tightened her lips and willed the crying away.

"Mama, I have money now! I'll go buy you some medicine!"

Her mother shook her head. "No, save the money. I'll be better soon. Don't worry about me."

Lillian made strong protests, but her mother shrugged them away. Finally she caressed the heavy bulge rising from her mother's belly. "How's this little one?"

Mama heaved a sigh and groped for words. Her whole body shuddered violently, and then she burst out, "I hate it! I wish it were all over!" A glistening teardrop squeezed out of each eye and she began coughing. "Third Uncle was right all along! I had to sell the machines. I sold them to that donkey Fat Old Wong! I sold Jin's dreams for firewood!"

Lillian held her mother's hands and massaged them. Oh, Mama, she pleaded silently, don't cry! She stood up. "I'll make you some tea."

But when she came back into the bedroom, Mama's eyes had closed. Lillian leaned over to listen to her laboured breathing and gently brushed her hair. She had never noticed how much grey was streaked through there. Oh, God, she prayed. Please make Mama strong enough to have this baby!

Lillian lay her hands on Mama's and felt the chill again. Her mother stirred slightly but slept on.

Suddenly Lillian sat down and straightened her back. Firmly shutting her eyes, she reached inside her blouse to feel the warmth that nestled above her belly. She wriggled her other hand into Mama, and then started to breathe the way Cariboo Wing had showed her.

Slowly and gently, the air came in and out. She listened and counted her breaths patiently, resolving to count into the millions. Gradually her fingers grew warmer.

This time the focussing came much more easily. She felt her entire being settle down to one centre. Dipping deep within, she tried to transform the anguish and anger of the last few days into strength and energy. She would make Mama well. She would give her mother courage and new hope and...

Time passed, but Lillian didn't feel it swift or slow. Memories came to her. Cariboo's words. Her parents laughing, a long time ago. Papa leaving. Mama slapping Third Uncle. Yiwen flying. The sick man on the cabin floor. Then she felt her mother's body shift. Opening her eyes, Lillian saw that she had awakened.

"Ah-Lai," Mama whispered. "I'm thirsty. And... and a bit hungry, too. Mrs. Chang, she brought over some rice soup this morning, but I couldn't eat then. Can you heat it up for me?"

Lillian leapt to obey. Her mother ate slowly but eagerly, even though she had to be fed one spoonful at a time. And when Mama was finished, a round glow lit her face, and she smiled weakly. "I feel better." Then she fell asleep once again.

In a daze, Lillian took the bowl downstairs to wash. Had her healing really worked? Had she really injected new strength into her mother?

Blind-Eye was sitting at the kitchen table, dozing. Suddenly he spoke up. "Ah-Lai, you did well."

She swung around in surprise.

"The blind hear more than just words," he added. "Your hay-gung will bring your mother back."

Lillian looked perplexedly at him.

"The heart that you took to the mountains," he continued, "was mightier than the head."

There was a moment of silence. Then Lillian took a deep breath. "Blind-Eye, Papa's dead." Saying the words aloud was like emptying a heavy pail of water that she had been carrying uphill for a long, long time.

Blind-Eye nodded, as if he had known all along. "He was a good man. And my dearest friend. May his soul rest, but his spirit live on."

Lillian turned and saw tears sliding down his face. She reached out and gripped his dry, gnarled hands.

"Papa will live on," she said fiercely.

"You'll carry on his fight?"

"Yes."

8

THOUGH the afternoon sky was swiftly darkening, the streets of Chinatown were still busy with the movement of people. Lillian came out of the family store and breathed deeply. Quickly she ran towards the broad, imposing building where the Athletic Club headquarters were located.

She stepped into the dim entrance, where a man sprang up and startled her. He was burly and heavy, wrapped in a thick padded jacket. "Where are you going?" he demanded, blocking her way.

"Upstairs, to the Athletic Club."

"They're busy today. Go somewhere else to play!"

"I didn't come to play!" protested Lillian. "I came to see Dr. Sun. I've got to talk to him!"

"Who said he was here?" challenged the guard. His thick lips pulled into an ugly sneer. He waited for Lillian to run off. "He's not here, I tell you!"

"Then let me go up and see!" Lillian moved to pass him, but he seized her arm.

"I told you to go somewhere else to play!" he snarled.

"I'm not playing!" Lillian cried. "Let go of me!"

He did, but by flinging her back so that she tripped and landed in a heap on the sidewalk. When she looked up, he towered over her with a hard glint in his eyes. Then, slowly, he opened his jacket and stuck his elbows out and his hands onto his waist. Lillian saw the sleek gun barrel peeking from his belt.

She quickly picked herself up and ran towards Canton Alley. She would have to forget about getting help from the Athletic Club. How about that other fellow, Lam, the one from China who had come to look for Papa and to check on Dr. Sun's safety? Maybe she could find him. The bakery was run by several Lams. Surely they would know where to find him.

"Who? Oh, you mean Little Lam!" cried the baker. "The big talker on the revolution, is that the one?"

Lillian nodded eagerly. "Where can I find him today?"

"Little Lam? He's busy right now. Dr. Sun's getting ready for his speech this afternoon, and Little Lam's organizing things. You'd think he was a general himself!" The baker cheerfully wiped his counter clean. "There was a meeting at the Wing Lung store, I think. Try there."

Lillian hurried out back onto the street, praying that Little Lam would be there. She passed by some men and heard them grumbling about being late for the big speech. It sounded like everyone in Chinatown was going.

She ran into the big general store. The wooden bins and matted baskets were heaped full of beans and groceries, but the aisles were empty of shoppers.

"Is Little Lam here?" she asked.

The clerk's eyes narrowed. "No, he's not here. Who said he was here?"

"Oh...I...no one." Lillian shrugged. "He must be at the Athletic Club, then." She retreated, but not before she caught the clerk's eye steal momentarily towards the back curtain.

Once outside, Lillian slid up by the storefront. With her cheek tight against the brick wall, she peeked back through the window into the store. The clerk was busy writing into a ledger. Passersby on the street sent curious glances in her direction.

Her cheeks and palms grew cold. Then a trio of men pushed by her and stalked into the store. Lillian's eyes gleamed. She peeked inside again and saw the customers send the clerk up a ladder in the back corner to fetch some goods. Quickly she darted inside and crept behind the counter like a cat.

Holding her breath tightly, she peered out at the men until they moved away. Then she slid towards the back, under the curtain and into the storeroom. Immediately the deep, sharp aroma of soya sauce filled her nose. She groped her way by some enormous urns and then saw Little Lam and two men clustered around an overturned box. Little Lam was busy with brush and ink, filling out forms while the other two men counted a huge stack of slips and recorded numbers in a ledger.

Taking a deep breath, Lillian stepped out from the dark.

"Excuse me, Mr. Lam. Do you have some time?"

The men spun around in surprise and Little Lam jumped to his feet.

"How did you get in here?" he demanded. "Who let you pass —"

"It's all right," soothed one of his co-workers. "It's just a girl."

The other fellow chortled, "*Mr.* Lam? Wah! Little Lam, you've hit the big times! No pretty girl ever calls me 'Mr.'! Not even when I pay her!"

Lillian's face reddened, but she boldly walked up to Lam. "Can I talk to you? Alone?" she asked quietly.

"Alone, she wants to talk with you alone," teased the fellow. "Hey, Little Lam, you'd better move fast!"

"You can talk to me here," Little Lam ordered. "These are my friends." He threw the ink-brush down and glared at Lillian. "What do you want?"

"It's about my father..." Her voice shook.

"He's back?"

"No...I...I don't think he's ever coming back," she finally managed.

"Could have told you that long ago," he replied curtly. "Where's the money?"

"I...I don't know." She looked wildly around and saw three pairs of accusing eyes converge on her.

"Ah, he's long gone," Little Lam announced. "Somewhere in the hills, there's one very rich man! Ho Jin Chong stole a fortune from the revolution and never came home!"

In a rage, Lillian spun around and ran blindly for the curtain just as two men were coming through. She crashed straight into them.

"What's this?" Lillian heard a voice cry out and someone swiftly pinned her arms down. "What's going on back here?"

Desperately she struggled against the strong hands holding her, and Little Lam came running up. "Nothing! It's just a girl, Dr. Sun. She was just —"

Dr. Sun?

"Dr. Sun, I've got to talk to you!" Lillian burst out. "My father didn't steal your money! It was stolen from him! He died for your revolution!"

"What's that? Who is this girl?" Lillian's captor released her, and she found herself staring into a strong, moustached face. Dr. Sun was dressed in a western suit. His hair was parted down the middle and smoothly slicked back. He glared at Little Lam.

"I asked you a question. Who is this girl?"

"She's Ho Jin Chong's daughter," Little Lam answered weakly.

"Ho Jin Chong was collecting for us," Dr. Sun's aide whispered to him. He held the curtain up to let light into the storeroom. "He disappeared a few months back and was never heard of again."

"Ah, I remember, I remember."

"He was murdered!" Lillian cried out. "By the Empire!"

Dr. Sun frowned. "How do you know this?"

"I heard my Third Uncle trying to sell Papa's notebook to another man. Third Uncle found out where Papa was travelling and sold the information to the Empire!"

"She's lying, Dr. Sun!" charged Little Lam. "She doesn't want to face the truth! Her father's a thief! All Chinatown knows that."

"No! That's not true!" insisted Lillian.

Dr. Sun's eyes stared coolly into hers. "Do you have any proof?"

"No...I...I have none, but..."

"This is rubbish!" interrupted the aide. "Dr. Sun, you're due to speak in half an hour. Let's go! We won't have another chance to meet such a large audience!"

"No, wait!" Lillian exclaimed. "I can get proof! There ...there must be a way..."

Dr. Sun looked at Lillian closely. "Sit down," he said gently. "Tell me everything..."

* * * *

The door of the Chinese Theatre hung open and the lobby lay empty. Lillian heard loud applause as she ran up the steps to the balcony. She burst out onto the darkened gallery and caught her breath. Every seat in the theatre was taken. Rows of spectators stood packed against the back. Men were even sitting on the stairway. The air hung thick with smoke from cigarettes and Sunday cigars.

She looked around and saw that she was the only female there. A few people turned to look at her. For the opera performances, women and children always sat in a separate room downstairs. The view from the upstairs made her feel as if she was floating high over the stage.

Gingerly she squeezed her way through the crowd until a clear view of the stage opened up. Then she stood up on her tiptoes and craned her neck forward. There was Dr. Sun standing alone on the brightly lit stage. She caught the glitter of a shiny watch chain dangling from his vest pocket.

"The Empire ignores the needs of the people," he shouted, striding from one side of the stage to the other with long steps. "Too many men and women are dying from the government's mistakes. The Chinese people want to be proud of their homeland! We want to stand tall in the world of nations! It's time to arm ourselves and fight our corrupt rulers!"

Lillian tore her eyes off the stage and peered around for Third Uncle. She scanned row after row of backs and heads, looking for a recognizable shape. But she couldn't spot him anywhere. She breathed deeply to fight off the panic. What if Third Uncle hadn't come tonight? What if he was drinking and eating at some teahouse?

Then she spotted a hat with a familiar sag. It was Third Uncle, sitting on the other side of the balcony.

Lillian's eyes settled on him as if he were the centre in a bull's-eye. He was whispering to his neighbour and then they laughed. Was that the agent from the Empire?

At that moment Dr. Sun thrust his fist into the air. "We must not be afraid!" he cried. "We cannot be afraid!" The audience rose to its feet in one wave, applauding loudly.

"No!" the crowd shouted in one unified voice. "No fear!"

"Our land will be strong! Our nation will know no fear!" shouted Dr. Sun.

"No fear! No fear!" came the loud response.

"Ten thousand years for China! Ten thousand years for China!"

Dr. Sun shouted out the traditional salute for long life, and the people roared, "Ten thousand! Ten thousand! Ten thousand years for China!"

Never before had Lillian heard the power of so many voices. She hopped up and down over the wildly waving crowd to watch Third Uncle closely. He was hunched over talking to his companion. She looked around for Little Lam, too, but he was nowhere to be seen. Then Dr. Sun gestured for everyone to sit down.

"The Chinese in this province of British Columbia," he said, "have been exceedingly generous in donating funds to the cause. Chinese living around the world are playing a vital role in the revolution! I thank you all deeply."

At that moment everything before Lillian's eyes

seemed to float by in slow motion. Dr. Sun reached into his jacket and pulled out a tattered notebook. It was the size of a small Bible. He held it up for the entire audience to see.

"This book is your monument!" he announced dramatically. "This is paper now, but soon it will be carved into stone! This book contains the names of every man and woman living in your province who has donated to the revolution. When we are victorious, and I know we will win, every name will be engraved in stone to mark them as a parent to the new China!"

The air filled with applause, but Dr. Sun asked for silence.

"But revolution is a life and death matter," he continued, dropping his voice. "The man who kept this notebook is someone that you know, someone from this city. That man died delivering this document to me. I paid a fortune to recover this notebook. But that money pales in comparison to the price that Ho Jin Chong paid. He paid with his life!"

The view before Lillian's eyes tilted dizzily as an uneasy murmur churned through the listeners. Dr. Sun raised his voice one final time. "I ask that we take up a special collection to help his family!"

A roar of approval swept through the theatre. Then Third Uncle's companion lurched to his feet like an angry ox and fought his way towards the exit. Third Uncle pulled frantically to stop him. Lillian drew herself behind the door and watched them turn into the staircase. Then she grabbed her skirts and raced down

the stairs on her side of the building. In the lobby, she glimpsed her uncle hobbling after his companion in a panic.

Where were Little Lam and his friends? They were supposed to be following Third Uncle to see if he might lead them to the real notebook!

"Wait, listen to me!" she heard Third Uncle screeching outside. "Wait, I say! It's a trick! Don't listen to him!"

Lillian darted out. It was dark now, and the only light came from stores and restaurant windows lining the street. She saw Third Uncle staggering and clawing after his friend at the end of the alley. She glanced back inside the lobby. Little Lam and his friends had still not shown up. She gritted her teeth and started after the two men.

The men had ducked into a narrow passageway between two tall buildings. Lillian peered around the corner and saw the heavy shadow trying to shake Third Uncle loose.

"Listen to me," she heard Third Uncle plead. "I still have the notebook! Old Sun has a fake! He's lying! They're trying to trick you!"

"Everyone's trying to trick me!" the agent shouted furiously. "So you did shop around for a higher price. And you found a better deal, didn't you? Give me back my advance money now!"

"I haven't got it," wailed Third Uncle.

"Money passes through you like water!" Suddenly the voice turned menacing, and Lillian saw her uncle back off. "Nobody makes a fool of me and lives to talk about it!"

"No, no..." she heard Third Uncle blubber for help. Fear crackled through his voice and sent chills down Lillian's spine. "You've been tricked! No! Don't!"

She saw the two dark figures grunt and grapple with each other. And before she could move, she heard Third Uncle groan loudly and crumple to the ground. The agent fled in the opposite direction, and then all fell quiet again.

Lillian ran up to the figure huddled in the dark.

"Third Uncle? Third Uncle?" she whispered urgently. There was no response. Was he dead? She bent over and pulled his head up to let some light from a faraway door fall on his face. Third Uncle's head lolled limply from side to side, and then he moaned.

She gasped with relief. He clutched frantically in the air and at his side. Then he caught her fingers and took them down to his stomach. Lillian felt a slimy warmth slither over her hands. It was blood. Third Uncle had been stabbed! She jerked back. She swallowed thickly to keep her rolling stomach calm and then slapped his face lightly.

"The notebook, where is it?" she whispered grimly. She brought her face close to his mouth where the foul odour of whisky rose. She shook him as roughly as she dared. "Third Uncle, tell me! Papa's notebook, the notebook of names, where did you put it?"

Her uncle winced, and then his whole body twitched in pain. "Ah-Lai? Is that you, Ah-Lai?" he croaked.

"Yes, it's me," replied Lillian urgently. "Tell me where you hid Papa's notebook!" She wanted to shake the answer from him.

"Save my life, save my life," he murmured. "I'm dying..."

She bent close to his ear. "Tell me where you hid Papa's notebook! Tell me now! Tell me or I won't help you."

Third Uncle's eyelids lifted briefly. "Behind Gwan Gung," he whispered. Then he fell limp in Lillian's arms.

Lillian rose and stared at the motionless bundle lying at her feet. She looked up and saw heavy brick walls frowning down upon her. Why should she help him? He had killed Papa. She could let him die and nobody would know. Not a single window opened out from either wall. There had been no witnesses.

With a groan, Lillian turned and ran down the alleyway, her footsteps clattering loud and hollow over the cobblestones.

9

LILLIAN burst into the herbalist's store with a shout.

"Come quickly!" she cried to the man dozing behind the counter. "Someone's been stabbed! He's dying!"

The storekeeper jerked awake and rummaged for bandages. Together they ran into the lane, where they found two policemen hovering over Third Uncle.

"Is...is he dead?" Lillian blurted out. She tiptoed forward cautiously.

The constables looked up and shook their heads. "No, he's still alive. We've sent for the wagon to take him to hospital."

Lillian glanced at the man sprawled on the ground and sagged in relief. Thank goodness someone else would take him away. She didn't want to decide if he lived or died.

With the herbalist, she turned and walked back towards the store.

"Ah-Lai, there you are!" shouted a voice from behind. Little Lam came running up. "We couldn't get out of the theatre," he puffed. "When Dr. Sun called for donations to your family, the entire audience pressed forward like a tidal wave. We couldn't move!" He looked around anxiously. "Where's your Third Uncle?"

"The policemen are taking him to the hospital. He was stabbed."

"Stabbed? And the notebook?"

"I know where it is," replied Lillian. "Come with me."

When they walked into Hing Kee, the storefront was blazing with light and filled with people. A crowd of men immediately surrounded Little Lam, clamouring that he accept their donations for the Hos. Many of them were Papa's former workers. Mrs. Chang spotted Lillian and quickly drew her upstairs.

"Oh, this is so tragic, Ah-Lai." She threw one arm around her shoulder. "Your poor mother. Your father was such a good man..."

The sitting room was filled with visitors who had come to offer condolences. Fat Old Wong was there, along with Chinatown's richer merchants who were the leaders of the community. They must have come straight from the theatre and sent word to their wives. Winnie and Nellie sat near the wall, sniffing and wiping at their eyes.

"Mama!" Lillian broke through the crowd of women hovering about and rushed over to her mother who was sitting dazedly at the table. She knelt and saw the dampness on her mother's cheeks. "Mama, are you all right?"

Mama opened her mouth, but only hoarse, broken whimpers came out. Lillian cupped her hands around her mother's and felt them stiff and damp. Desperately she massaged them. "Mama, you're all right, aren't you? Say something!"

"Hush, don't make so much noise!" Mrs. Chang came up and pulled Lillian's hands away. "Leave her alone for now. I steamed some chicken broth with ginger. Once she drinks that, she'll be fine."

"But..."

The women of Chinatown closed in around Mama as if she were a sick child. Two of them gripped Lillian's shoulders and propelled her towards the door. "Look at Ah-Lai! She doesn't even cry! What a strong one she is!"

Lillian angrily shoved the arms away. Who did these women think they were? Where had they been when Mama really needed help?

"Ah-Lai." Behind Lillian, Little Lam's voice was quiet but urgent. "The notebook..."

Suddenly the commotion in the room stopped as a new arrival stood at the door of the sitting room. It was Dr. Sun.

Lillian brushed Lam aside and turned back to her mother. Mama's eyes had softened into pools of water. Her arms were wrapped tightly around her belly, as if she were bitterly cold. Lillian pulled the shawl up over her mother's shoulder and felt a slight tremor shake her body.

"Mama," she whispered. "It's Dr. Sun. He's here."

Mama's eyes blazed, and then she shrugged. "What do I care?"

Dr. Sun knocked gently at the open door. "May I come in?"

Mama's helpers scurried for his hat and coat while the men quickly stood up. The chairs scraped and clattered. Visitors bowed and nodded their heads rapidly in respect and greeting. "Hello, Doctor. You're well, Doctor."

He gestured for everyone to relax. "Please, sit down, sit down. We're all amongst our own people."

When the chairs were rearranged in a tight circle around the stove, everyone waited in an uncomfortable silence. Dr. Sun sat beside Mama. Finally he cleared his throat and said quietly, "Mrs. Ho, your husband was a very brave man."

Mama glanced up dully. "Brave men are fools."

"That may be so," Dr. Sun nodded. "But the world still needs such people."

Mama shook her head. "You speak of people, I speak of one man. One man with a family, with a baby about to be born."

Dr. Sun paused and let silence settle over the room. Lillian looked up as Blind-Eye pushed his way through the crowd pressing at the doorway. Word had spread rapidly about the Hos' famous visitor.

"Ho Jin Chong's family *was* important to him," Dr. Sun offered gently. "But he also saw the whole country as part of his family. He was concerned with the futures of countless babies when he undertook this work."

"You are a man who can talk," Mama stated, looking straight at Dr. Sun. "You have ideas that excite men, you have followers all over the world. I am just one woman, trying to raise a family. I feel betrayed. Jin should have married the revolution, not a woman!"

Lillian's heart went out to her mother. Mama was right. But Papa had been right, too.

The doctor had no reply and looked up gratefully when Mrs. Chang held out a cup of tea. He took a long sip of the hot liquid and tipped his head at Lillian.

"You were right about everything! It's a good thing that I listened to you."

Lillian nodded shyly. But Mama overheard.

"Right about everything? Right about what, Ah-Lai?" she demanded.

Lillian hesitated. "I...I told Dr. Sun that Third Uncle had...had betrayed Papa. But the only proof I could think of was the notebook. So I asked Dr. Sun to try to get it back by waving a fake one in front of Third Uncle."

"What? You knew?" Mama groped for words. "But...how?"

"Third Uncle stole a letter Papa sent to us. I found it. And Cariboo Wing told me how important the notebook was. Then I overheard Third Uncle trying to sell it."

Mama's face crumpled as she cried out bitterly, "Stupid girl, why didn't you tell me? Why was I the last to know?"

The visitors muttered uneasily as Mrs. Chang hurried to Mama's side.

"You were sick, Mama!" Lillian protested. "I was afraid for you and the baby."

Dr. Sun pulled out an envelope and laid it on the table.

"This sum was collected at tonight's meeting," he told Mama. "Everyone knows that Ho Jin Chong was a good man."

Mama stared dully at the envelope but did not move. Dr. Sun turned back to Lillian.

"Will you be returning to China?" he asked.

She gulped nervously. "I . . . I guess so. Mama's sold the machines downstairs to buy the tickets."

"But do you want to go to China?"

Lillian wriggled uncomfortably.

Then Mama spoke up. "What *do* you want, Ah-Lai?" she demanded loudly. "We may as well talk it over now."

Lillian looked around at all the faces staring intently at her. "I'll go wherever you go."

"Tell the truth!" her mother barked. "Do you want to go to China?"

"I . . . I . . ." Lillian looked away.

But Mama waited. "Well?"

Lillian took a deep breath and answered firmly. "No, I don't *want* to go. But I'll go."

Mama sighed long and hard. "I thought you'd make it easy for me," she said in a defeated tone. "I thought you'd tell me to stay here. I thought you hated China."

"Well, I did," Lillian admitted slowly. "Mostly I was scared of China. But not so much now as before."

Mama stared blindly into the wall. Finally she announced, "If you're not afraid of China, I'm not afraid of Canada. We'll stay." Then she shut her eyes wearily and leaned back into her chair.

Lillian couldn't believe her ears. They were going to stay! Maybe Mama did understand.

But Fat Old Wong rushed over. "You can't mean that," he protested. "Do you know what you're saying?"

Mama nodded without even opening her eyes.

His wife tottered over on her tiny bound feet. "Don't be foolish," she said, nudging at Mama's shoulder. "The Benevolent Association will pay your way to China, do you know that?"

"You're just a woman, don't forget," Fat Old Wong reminded her sternly. "Do you really think that you can raise a family by yourself here?"

Mama opened her eyes slowly. "I know I am just a woman," she answered serenely. "And I can do more here. Do you think that a girl in China could have done what Ah-Lai did? What Ah-Lai thinks and does, it comes from growing up in Canada. And that's enough for me to stay!"

* * * *

After all the adult farewells were said and done, Dr. Sun and Little Lam walked with Lillian to the door of the sitting room.

"Are you glad to be staying in Canada?" Dr. Sun asked.

"Oh, yes!" Lillian replied happily. "With the money from my job and hand-sewing jobs coming in here, our family will do fine!"

Dr. Sun looked at her closely. "Don't you feel anything for China?"

"I...I guess I do," she faltered. "I do...but China's too far away. It's...it's a country I don't know. I'd have to start all over if we went there. But here, I can do things!"

"Here you can make your father's dreams come true, too," the doctor added gently. "Do you have the notebook?"

Lillian nodded and led Dr. Sun and Little Lam downstairs. From the kitchen she dragged an old crate over to Gwan Gung's shelf and climbed up to the little altar.

The stern, crimson-faced god sat with his legs set sturdily apart as if astride a horse. He wore a military helmet, but one hand held an open book. Underneath his open robe was a metal chestplate and a warrior's armour. Gwan Gung combined the wisdom and skills gleaned from both books and the martial arts. Merchants, poets and fighters alike would burn incense and candles before his image to summon his spirit into their homes.

Lillian thrust her hand behind the screen where Gwan Gung's weapons rested and rummaged around. Her hands closed around a bundle and she brought it down. It didn't look like much — just a black-covered copy book tied together with string. She turned it over in her hand and felt it throb with life. Without a word, she handed the notebook to Dr. Sun.

"Thank you, Lillian," Dr. Sun said. He looked at the notebook closely and whispered, "Thank you, Jin."

His eyes rested on Lillian again. "You're part of a new generation, Lillian. I don't pretend to understand you Chinese who are born overseas. So good luck and goodbye. I'll remember Vancouver well." He turned and went out the front door.

"Goodbye," murmured Lillian. She stood still for a second. Suddenly the strangest question popped into her head. She darted outside. "Dr. Sun, wait!"

He turned, and Lillian ran up to him. "Dr. Sun," she blurted out. "Can people really fly? Can a woman jump to the rooftops like in the sword stories?"

Dr. Sun's moustache pulled back into a grin. "I've heard of those stories, too." He leaned close and nodded. "And I believe them. If the heart's in the right place and the body is trained, you can soar to any height you want!"